Untamed
FATE

VERACITY OF THE GODS
BOOK 2.5

K. D. MILLER

ISBN: 979-8-9991824-0-1

For Lexie, Kayleigh, and Kayla - thank you for bullying me relentlessly for this book.
And yes, Zeus is effing coming, alright?

....that's what she said

CHAPTER
ONE

"Long ago, before the notion of time as mortals know it even existed, before most worlds were even specks of dust in the ether, there were the Fates. Five powerful, mystical beings with the gift—and curse—of seeing all that would come to be. All possibilities. All outcomes. A fluid, ever-changing tapestry that stretched on into eternity. In the beginning, they had no names, simply calling each other *brother* or *sister*, though only two of them were truly siblings. Twins, born of the same soul, as close as any two beings could be. Eventually, the world changed, as it always does, and the gods came to be, worlds within worlds were formed, mortals and supernaturals were created and the tapestry grew ever longer, ever more complicated and confusing and beautiful.

The Fates came to be called Zerafina, Aamon, Magera, Emmeralda, and Allister. They all looked very different, physically: Zerafina was tall and lithe, with alabaster skin and flaming red hair, her eyes a cold, brittle black; Aamon was short and brawny, with olive skin, golden hair, and kind, silver eyes; Magera was voluptuous, with hair black as night and eyes like green flames; Emmeralda's skin was a warm brown while her twin's was more bronze, but they were identical when it came to their silver hair and purple eyes. Despite their physical differences, the Fates all shared the power to see and read the tapestry, as well as wielding other great magics. Some were stronger than others...

One much, *much* stronger.

For eons, they watched the future, and recorded what quickly became the past. It was an important life, but a lonely one. They came to settle on an island within the sky kingdom of Empyrean, where the King of the Gods, a handsome devil named Zeus, resided. Though they were technically part of Empyrean, the Fates rarely interacted with anyone outside of their island. Hermes, the Messenger God came with news or to take messages, but they rarely had other visitors. Their duty was one that was held as the most sacred and important, and therefore, their focus should *only* be on the future, on the tapestry—not on relationships, or friendships, or other silly things that gods and mortals entertained themselves with.

The Fates were to watch, not to interfere. Even so, Zeus began to come to the island more and more often, seeking guidance or attempting to flirt his way to having the future revealed to him and gaining insight into how to steer an outcome in a certain direction. Emmeralda and Allister secretly loved when Zeus or Hermes visited, were drawn to the interactions more so than the others.

But the Fates were forbidden from dalliances, from romance or marriage or love. Emmeralda often wondered who, exactly, they were forbidden *by*, but she kept her questions to herself. She knew there was something else out there, some nameless, faceless entity that held unimaginable power over even the Fates.

Though they had each other, it was a lonely existence.

Zerafina, Aamon, and Magera did not seem to mind...did not seem to feel much of anything, really. Aamon and Magera had flits of it here and there, their feelings surging as they watched some beings' future, but it always passed. Emmeralda wondered if it was because the feelings truly ebbed and flowed, or if Aamon and Magera were simply afraid of Zarafina's condemnation. Zerafina was hard and cold at all times, never seeming to feel anything but a sense of duty and superiority.

But Emmeralda and Allister were built differently. They felt *too* much. They both watched the futures of an infinite number of souls, watched love and death and joy and hate and agony—and *felt* it. Longed for it. Grew envious of those who experienced such things.

It was a day unlike any other when everything changed.

Emmeralda was watching the river of the tapestry as it flowed through the temple at the heart of their island when she gasped, jolting upright as if she'd been shocked. She threw out a hand to pull out a single thread of the tapestry and examine it more closely. Surely she hadn't seen what she thought she had...

But yes. There, in the vision, was *Allister*. Allister happy and laughing and in love with the Messenger God. A thousand emotions washed over Emmeralda like a great wave of Poseidon's making: wonder, happiness, confusion, love, even jealousy.

Allister entered the temple then, the others behind him. Emmeralda whirled, the thread still in her hands and tears in her eyes.

"Are you alright?" Allister asked, immediately knowing that something was going on with his twin.

"Yes," she breathed, wanting so badly to throw her arms around him, to tell him how happy she was for him, how much she loved him—all for something that had not happened yet. Aamon, Magera and Zerafina fanned out into a loose line. Aamon and Magera studied Emmeralda with confusion and interest, Zerafina with suspicion and malice. Zerafina's eyes narrowed on the thread in Emmeralda's hands, and then flew wide.

She'd seen.

Quicker than any being, mortal or otherwise, could track, Emmeralda lashed out with her power, ropes of silver, shimmering energy encircling her brother and pulling him behind her with one rough tug. Aamon and Magera cried out in confusion, cowering to the side as Zerafina raised her hands, her own deep green power sparking in her palms.

"Do. Not. Touch. Him," Emmeralda said in a low, even voice laced with power and threat.

"It is forbidden!" Zerafina nearly shrieked. "It cannot be!"

"What? What is happening?" Allister demanded, confusion and apprehension coloring his voice.

Magera gasped softly as she looked at the thread, still hovering above the tapestry.

"Love?" she whispered. A soft, almost wistful smile pulling her full lips upward.

Emmeralda saw Allister turn out of the corner of her eye—she didn't dare take her gaze off of Zarafina—and stare at the thread. His jaw went slack as confusion washed over him.

"That's...that's me..." He raised a hand, as if to reach out and stroke the thread, but quickly dropped it back to his side, his fingers curling into a fist. "Alda," he whispered the name he alone called her, "what's going on?"

"We are leaving," Emmeralda said simply.

"What?!" four voices rang out in unison. Three in confusion, one in incredulous rage.

"Allister and I shall be Fates no more. We shall leave this island and live among the gods and other immortals. The Fates will now be three." Allister tensed beside her.

"Alda—"

"You cannot simply leave," Zerafina snapped, cutting Allister off with a sneer. "It isn't possible."

"It is and we are," Emmeralda said, unyielding surety in her voice. When Zerafina's eyes flashed, Emmaralda let her power flow more strongly through her. Waves of energy shot out around her, her eyes turning wholly silver and the runes on her skin burning brightly. The sky above the temple darkened and an ethereal wind blew around them. Zerafina's eyes widened and she swallowed hard as she took an involuntary step backwards. Despite being the self-appointed leader of the Fates, she knew that Emmeralda was far more powerful.

Aamon and Magera huddled together, quickly retreating into a corner, eyes wide.

"Emmeralda, you cannot," Zerafina said, though her voice was not nearly as sharp as it was before.

"You know that I can, Zerafina. If you try to stop us from leaving, I will kill you all." Emmeralda's voice was unwavering, her conviction set in stone. She tilted her head to the side and raised a hand into the air. A new thread from the tapestry rose up and the others all gasped in horror. Emmeralda knew what they were seeing, as the vision had just flashed through her own mind as well: their bodies, lifeless on the ground of this temple, blood pooling around them and staining the white stone; the tapestry turning from a smoothly flowing river into a violent whirlpool; the balance of everything in the world on a razor's edge of chaos. But Emmeralda loved her brother enough to risk everything for his chance at happiness and love.

"Alright!" Zerafina yelled. "Alright," she said again, softer, a defeated slump to her shoulders. The thread wavered and dissolved completely as that outcome vanished, changed forevermore by the decision that had just been made. The others let out gasps of relief. "Is this what you want, Allister? The choice should be yours, not hers," she said, pointedly curling her lip in Emmeralda's direction.

Allister glanced between Zerafina, Emmeralda, and the thread. His breath seemed to catch in his throat as he watched the thread, the potential future he had. None of the Fates had ever seen their own futures before—because none of them *had* real futures to speak of. They were *of* the world, but not a *part* of it, not truly.

But now, Allister could be.

And perhaps, Emmeralda could be as well.

"Yes," he breathed. "Yes, this is what I want." He rubbed the heel of his hand against his chest. "I have felt...I did not know it was love that was blooming in my chest over these years that Hermes has been visiting the island. But now, I understand. And I want a chance to explore it, to truly feel it."

And just like that, a thousand new threads flared to life within the tapestry, ones that Emmeralda knew she was a part of, though she couldn't see herself completely clearly within them. A new life for them both, full of love and loss and laughter and tears. And thousands of other new threads, new paths formed by their new places within the world.

"And if it ends like so many futures we have seen?" Zerafina asked harshly. "If your heart breaks because of this love?" She spit the word as if it were poison.

Allister swallowed hard, but straightened his shoulders, reaching out to grasp Emmeralda's hand. Her power surged higher as it combined with her twin's. His own power flared out around them both as well, joining the swirling tempest. Together, the others were no match.

"It will be worth any pain that may come. You will not dissuade our decision."

After a tense moment, Aamon and Magera watching raptly from the corner, Zerafina finally sighed in defeat.

"Fine. Go. But you will never be able to return here. You will truly be Fates no more. You will be...other. Immortal, yes, but unlike any other beings in any of the worlds. Your powers will remain, as will your foresight, though I do not know how strong it will be without our collective power being shared. I..." She cocked her head to the side as she studied the tapestry behind Emmeralda. She knew it must be changing and shifting as different futures spread out before them. Whatever Zerafina saw made her exhale roughly, whatever biting words she'd had on her tongue fading away. "I wish you well," she said instead, sounding resigned.

"Mind yourself, Emmeralda," she added quietly as Emmeralda and Allister moved to leave the temple, "you cannot control it all... though it appears you will try."

There was the tiniest bit of exasperated amusement in her voice.

Emmeralda would have millennia to study those words, to under-stand what they might mean...though interfering and trying to steer things *did* sound like something she would like to do...

And so it was that five Fates became three, that Allister found love, and, in the end, heartbreak, that Emmeralda found—"

"Uhh, Emmie...?" a voice cut in. Emmie snapped her eyes to the couch where Skylar sat, a cell phone in her hand. "This is a really cool story and all, but, uh, I asked what you wanted on your pizza...?"

Skylar gave Emmie a look that she'd had grown very used to seeing, one that clearly said *you are my best friend and I love you, but you are fucking crazy sometimes.*

"Oh." Emmie shrugged off the memories, coming back into the present. She gave Skylar a wide smile. "Pineapple and bacon. Of course."

Thirty minutes later, she, Skylar, Lucas, and Dean (in cat form) ate pizza in Lucas' huge loft apartment. It was a perfect mix of upscale modern bachelor pad, and cozy rustic hunting lodge. It really shouldn't work, but somehow it did. It was just so...Luke. His wolfy ties to the earth mixing with the high-class tastes he'd acquired—*earned*—through years of hard work with Willow Corp.

"So, you were seriously a *Fate*?" Skylar asked around a mouth full of crust that she'd stolen from Luke's plate. Luke had scowled, but Skylar merely winked at him and grinned. Now, his eyes flew wide.

Emmie rolled her eyes, tossing him a napkin just before he sputtered.

"What??" he gasped, nearly choking and successfully spilling beer all down his front. He took the napkin, giving her one of those looks that was somewhere between wary, amused, and impressed. He was still getting used to being around someone who could see the future, but was mostly taking it all in stride. He'd only just learned that the gods were real—not just real, but very much still alive and well—and he was already hanging out with them on the reg without much fuss. Lucas McBride was resilient, that was for sure.

He wiped his chin and tossed the napkin on the countertop

before standing. Emmie barely contained her gasp as he pulled his wet shirt over his head without hesitation. She saw most things before they happened, but not *everything*. For instance, Luke standing there in low-riding jeans, shirtless, his sculpted chest and abs slightly damp with beer she wanted to lick off, was *not* something she had seen or could ever fully be prepared for.

-*My Gods*- Dean said in her head, admiring the view right alongside her. -*That should be illegal, shouldn't it?*-

Dean, once upon a time known as Conan, could communicate telepathically with most of the gods and goddesses in the different Planes, but that power was now shared with Skylar and Lucas as well. He could speak with all of them at once, or single each person out, which came in handy since the three of them, and Skylar when she was available and not doing Queen of the Underworld things, were working hard to find the enchantress who had cursed him to his feline state—only she could remove the damn thing.

Dean was special to her, always had been. He was one of the first beings to befriend her after she and Allister had left the Fates. They'd been moving towards something even stronger than friendship when he'd been cursed and turned into a cat. She hadn't gone a minute without loving him all these years, and wondered if once the curse was lifted, they could rekindle the flame that had once burned.

Well, she'd wondered until she'd had a vision at Hades and Skylar's wedding celebration months earlier. The vision had stopped her in her tracks, both with the intensity of it and what she'd seen: *herself*. She never saw visions of her own future. In fact, she sometimes only knew for sure that she survived a particularly dicey situation because she saw herself on the fringes of someone *else's* future. But in this vision, it had undoubtedly been *her* future.

The vision had been...well, she didn't want to dwell on that now, but in it, she'd been calling out for Dean, reaching for him with a desperate longing, a love that made her chest ache. But she wasn't only reaching for Dean in that moment...

Now she let her gaze sweep lazily over Luke's body, over every hard plane and enticing hollow, every inch of smooth skin that she longed to touch and lick.

-*Get in line*- Dean said in her mind again, making her chuckle. Dean had always enjoyed both women and men, something not uncommon among immortal beings. It was only the mortals who thought that it was anything to even think twice about, let alone get into a huff over. What did someone's physical and emotional bonds and preferences have to do with anyone other than that person? Nothing. The answer was absolutely fucking nothing. Mortals had come a long way in the eons Emmie had watched them come into being, growing and changing with each century that passed, but they still had far to go in many areas.

She sighed as Luke walked out of the kitchen, admiring the sight of his bare back. *It would look good with scratches down it*, she thought, and then quickly forced the thoughts away.

"Yes, I was. It isn't that big of a deal," Emmie said, shrugging her shoulders.

"Not a big...Are you kidding me?" Luke called from the laundry room just off the kitchen, searching for a new shirt.

"It isn't. It was a long time ago and dreadfully boring. I hardly even remember it." Not entirely true, but she waved them away when they began to protest. "Anyway, another day in the archives tomorrow, then?" she asked, changing the subject.

-*Joy*- Dean said to everyone.

"Yeahhhh, I'm going to pass on archives duty, but you have fun with that," Skylar said, taking a swig of beer. Luke came back into the room, tugging a black t-shirt over his head. His big arms stretched the fabric, as did his chest. Most shifters were physically larger even when in their human form, but wolves were always especially brawny, and Luke was no exception.

"You're dipping out—*again*?"

"I am not! I have things to do. Very important things..."

"Hades is not an important thing, Pop Rocks," Emmie said pointedly.

"I'm sure he will love to hear that," Skylar said dryly.

"Well, he *is*," Emmie amended, "but boning him does not count as an important thing you need to do in order to get out of research." She loved Hades, loved all of her boys, as she affectionately called the three brothers. Skylar merely waggled her eyebrows and shrugged as if to say *sorry bout it, sorry for it, but I'm getting mine.*

"Well, since some people can't seem to keep it in their pants," Luke said, giving Skylar a pointed look, "looks like it'll just be the three of us again." The thought made Emmie's chest flutter. Though the archives were dank and dusty and not all that fun really, being with Dean and Lucas never failed to make her happy.

"Don't hate me 'cause you ain't me," Skylar said, downing the rest of her beer. "Alright, I'm outta here. I think I need to do those important things tonight as well, come to think of it." She winked and Dean laughed inside their minds. "Emmie, you coming?"

"You could stay," Luke said, a little too eagerly, and then ran a hand through his hair. "I mean, I've got that stack of books that I brought back yesterday. We could go through those. The three of us," he added, looking at Dean, "unless you want to go..."

-I'm good to stay-

"I'll stay for a while too. Poseidon is...busy," Emmie said, lips curling upwards knowing just what he was busy with. He was figuring out how to deal with his growing feelings for the alluring and mysterious Beck. There were some whoppers coming out of the woodworks with that one, but for now, they were both dancing around the giant elephant in the room.

"And Zeus is in a bad mood." He was dealing with his own inner turmoil over their friend Zahara. Emmie's smile widened as flashes of the future shuffled through her mind. Zeus was in for quite a ride soon.

Emmie actually had her own private—and mostly secret—realm she could go to, but it had a couple of occupants at the moment, so she was more than happy to stay with Luke and Dean.

"Alright then. Smell ya later, losers!" With that, Skylar flashed devil horns with her hands and phased away, disappearing completely. They all laughed, shaking their heads at the spot where Skylar had been a moment ago.

"Well, shall we?" Emmie asked, gesturing towards the leather couch where a mountain of books sat on the coffee table.

They made their way over, Dean winding his way between their legs, and they spent the rest of the night with their noses stuck in books. After an hour or so of reading, Luke got up to get another beer, rubbing his eyes on the way to the fridge.

"Hey, so how come this enchantress queen knew about the gods in the first place? Or did she not know who or what you were when she cursed you?"

-She didn't know what I was. I tended to...mingle more than some of the other gods and demigods in those days. An enchantress coven needed some assistance with a battle, prayed to the gods for aid, so some of us volunteered to go and fight. I stuck around afterwards for a bit-

"That's code for he stayed for the copious amounts of thank you sex," Emmie said with a smirk. She supposed she could have been jealous or upset at the time, but they hadn't made any kind of declarations to each other before he left for that fight. They were friends with the undeniable fires of more just below the surface, but they hadn't taken any official steps. So, she couldn't blame him for enjoying the spoils of war, so to speak. She could call him an idiot for centuries over it, of course, but she couldn't fault him for it.

-Hey, post-battle lust is a very real thing-

"He's right. It is," Luke agreed, settling back on the couch and offering Emmie another bottle.

-See, the pup knows-

Luke rolled his eyes at the nickname, but his lips tugged up at the corners as he went back to reading.

"I think I found something!" Lucas called from one of the tables in the archives. The room was beneath the mansion-slash-headquarters building where Skylar had grown up, but was magically extended to go on for miles and, for reasons Luke had never understood, was built like the catacombs in some movie set in medieval times. The walls were cold, rough stone, the floors the same stone but polished smooth, with low ceilings and cobwebs despite the fact that a cleaning crew routinely came through the place. Rows and rows of wooden shelves ran the length of the almost never-ending space, long tables set at intervals. Lights were attached to the walls like old torches, though they were electric, and each table had two massive lamps to provide more light for reading.

Dalton Pembroke had been collecting knowledge and artifacts and books long before he started Willow Corp. After he started recruiting, bringing in more species from more factions of the supernatural world, they all brought their own knowledge and artifacts and books, and soon, it was out of control. Hence the need for a magically extended space. Some factions even paid Willow Corp to store their histories within their archives, as it was one of the most secure places in all the world.

Or, well, the Mortal Plane at least. Lucas was still wrapping his head around all of this gods and goddesses and different planes and realms thing. It was...a lot. He could barely believe that Skylar was actually a demigoddess, let alone the fucking Queen of the Underworld and married to Hades. Like *the* Hades. Despite meeting the God numerous times, Luke admittedly couldn't think about him without picturing the guy with the blue hair from the cartoon movie. Not that he would ever admit that to Hades, himself, of course. He was scary as fuck when he wanted to be and Luke never, ever wanted to be on the receiving end of his full fury.

Dean jumped onto the table in front of Luke, making him tense in surprise.

"I'm getting you a fucking bell," he grumbled, glaring. The damned cat was silent as death. Though, of course, he wasn't truly a cat at all. He was a demigod who'd been cursed to *look* like a cat. As soon as Skylar had suggested that the key to ending his curse may very well be found in the archives and she'd introduced Dean and Lucas, he'd liked the guy. Or the cat. Or whatever. Sure, it had taken Lucas a little bit of time to get past the initial shock and confusion of the whole talking-to-a-cat-who's-talking-back-inside-my-head thing, but he'd actually gotten over it surprisingly quickly.

Dean was funny and sarcastic and a warrior to his core. That part of him called directly to Lucas, and they'd talked weapons and battle tactics for hours one of the first times he'd come to the archives, neither one of them realizing it was nearly morning until Luke's alarm had gone off—telling him it was time to wake up. Luke felt a kinship with Dean unlike anything he'd ever felt before, and had thrown himself into the task of searching for scraps of information on the possible whereabouts of the enchantress responsible for the curse.

She wasn't just any enchantress, she was their *queen*—and she'd been missing for centuries. Finding her wouldn't only mean lifting

Dean's curse, it would mean the entire faction would be indebted to Willow Corp, which equaled a huge payday and magical IOUs for the rest of eternity.

-*What's up, pup?*- Dean asked, pointedly ignoring the bell comment, but somehow looking smug in his cat form.

Lucas rolled his eyes at that. Dean just loved to downplay Luke's wolfiness and call him a puppy, as if he were just some overgrown Golden Retriever when he changed. He was terrifying, damn it. Men had literally pissed themselves at the sight of him in his wolf form on more than one occasion. He knew he was overreacting because a part of him admittedly felt very...inadequate now that he knew gods and demigods and Fates were real, and he seemed to be constantly surrounded by them. He couldn't help wondering if they looked down on him or found him lacking. Of course, he didn't *really* believe they thought that, but the doubts still crept in sometimes.

Emmie strolled up, looking downright sinful in a long, flowing gown that looked like it was made out of a lavender cloud, the purple only a few shades lighter than her eyes. Some days, Emmie dressed like a Grecian princess. Others, like a warrior queen. Still others, like a twenty-something going to Starbucks or a concert. She looked equally beautiful in every incarnation. She could change far more than her clothes, literally transforming into anyone on the planet, but Luke wouldn't change a single thing about her.

Light brown skin covered in shimmering silver tattoos that glowed when she used her power—which rivaled even the gods' and was honestly a little terrifying, though Luke hadn't even seen the full extent of it—violet eyes and silver hair. She was tall and willowy, and almost seemed to glide when she walked. *Perfect*, he thought. *She's fucking perfect.*

Luke clenched his fists and forced himself to focus on the task at hand, which was becoming harder and harder to do. He and Emmie had something going on. He wasn't sure what, yet, but it was something intense. They had a connection that he didn't completely understand, truth be told. It almost felt like she might be...his. His mate, though the instincts that should be rearing up inside him and making it absolutely clear that she was his were...off somehow. They were flaring, but they were telling him that more was to come, telling him that the mating bonds weren't completely snapping into place yet, and he didn't understand it at all. He was blaming the fact that she was entirely other and figured his instincts just had no idea what to do with that. Mates from different species weren't unheard of, but Luke didn't think any shifter had ever had a mate that was something as close to as a goddess as you could get without actually being one.

So, yeah, his instincts were probably just in a bit of a *WTF* state.

"What did you find?" she asked, jumping up to sit on the table just beside him, the long slit in her dress baring her thigh nearly up to her hip. Luke gnashed his teeth and forced his eyes away from her skin. Skin he wanted to touch, to taste, to grip and caress and— *stop it!*

She smiled and reached out to run her hand down Dean's back. Even as a cat, Luke could tell how much Dean loved the touch—and how strongly he felt for Emmie. Despite being an animal, his eyes were so intelligent, so telling. Luke was pretty sure Dean had been in love with Emmie for at least a few centuries, probably longer. Which, could get awkward seeing as how Luke was heading that direction as well. He tried not to think about it too much, to wonder who she might choose if given the chance...

Luke cleared his throat.

"I found something here about an old goblin cult who worshiped one of the first and most ruthless Enchantress Queens, Valen."

"Oh, I knew her!" Emmie said with a smile. "She was a vicious little creature. I once saw her enchant a man to dig his own eyeballs from his skull with a spoon and then eat them, only to have them grow back and he would start the process all over again. For years and years..." She laughed lightly but then seemed to realize the looks of alarm on Luke and Dean's faces. "He totally deserved it," she added hastily. "I mean, she was a Grade A bitch and a little psycho before being psycho was a thing, but this particular guy definitely deserved it. Promise. An-y-wayyyy, it would make sense that a cult would worship her."

-*So, what makes you think this has anything to do with Sabina?*- asked Dean, black tail flicking back and forth.

"Well, I remember reading something before about enchantress bloodlines, and it was believed that Sabina was a direct descendent of Valen."

Emmie's eyes widened. "So, the cult may very well have been keenly interested in her if they found out she was of Valen's line. They may even believe that she's Valen reincarnated!" Then she frowned. "But, I've never heard of this cult. Are they even still around?"

"Not sure," Luke said, "but it looks like they don't reside here in the Mortal Plane." That was still so weird to think about, let alone say. "Any idea where Drackenthul is?"

-*Yes*- Dean said at the same time Emmie said, "not a clue."

"How do you know where it is?" Luke asked, looking at Dean with an arched brow.

-*I did some bounty hunting there once for Hera.*-

"Can you get us back there?" Emmie asked, excitement flaring in her eyes.

-*I think so, yeah, but be prepared: it's not the most pleasant realm*-

Luke grinned at the cat. "Should be fun, then."

Emmie clapped her hands and smiled widely.

"Vacay time!"

Dean couldn't believe that they'd finally found an actual lead after all this time. He could hardly remember what it felt like to be in his true body. He'd nearly gone mad more than once over the years trapped in this form, had even contemplated giving up completely. If he could not live as a man, then he didn't want to live at all. But every time those thoughts arose, Emmie would show up, seeing his potential future ending abruptly, and talk him out of it. Sometimes with words, sometimes just by simply sitting with him in the silence and reminding him by her mere presence that he was stronger than this, that he could endure. She couldn't ever tell him when, exactly, or give any details, but she knew that one day the curse *would* be lifted, he just needed to hold on.

He'd always hoped that if they could end this damned curse, then perhaps they could continue what they began nearly a thousand years ago. And he still wanted it. He wanted it so damn badly that his soul ached for her, but now there was a complication.

And his name was Lucas McBride.

"Alright, I think that's everything," Luke said, zipping the pack he'd placed on Emmie's slim shoulders before tugging on his own and strapping a pistol to his thigh, a dagger at his belt, and crossing two swords into sheaths just beneath the pack against his back.

"Dean," Luke said.

Dean. He liked the way the name rolled off of Luke's tongue, the low rumble of his voice. It had been nearly four hundred years since Emmie had looked at him, said, "you're going to be Dean one day. I'll go ahead and start calling you that to get you used to it," and had done just that. She'd been the only one of course, everyone else usually being confused as hell when she said it, but he had kind of liked it. It had been like a secret that only the two of them shared. So, he'd felt like Dean for a long time now. When Skylar finally showed up in the Underworld and decided that he reminded her of Dean Winchester, it all finally clicked into place, and now everyone had caught onto the name.

"I couldn't find a cat-sized backpack, but I did find this adorable little bandana..." Luke said, bending down and holding a red paisley-printed bandana out towards him.

Dean hissed and swatted the material away, making Luke grin like a dickhead.

-Do you know how hard it is to get the smell of cat piss out of your underwear drawer, pup? Care to find out?-

"Ok, ok," Luke said, holding his palms up in surrender, "no bandana. Can I interest you in this cute little collar? It has duckies on it..."

With that, Dean launched himself at Luke, using his claws to climb up Luke's body, scratching as he went, moving too quickly for Luke to catch, despite his attempts. He shot over Luke's chest and shoulders, down his back, around again and again as Luke spun and yelped. When Dean sank his little fangs into Luke's ear and the shifter bellowed, Emmie finally stopped laughing long enough to intervene.

"Ok, that's enough! Both of you."

"He bit me!" Luke whined, glaring at Dean when he hopped lightly down to the ground.

-And I'll do it again, pup-

"You deserved it," Emmie said and then turned her gaze on Dean. "And you—behave."

-Fine.- Dean said, smirking (as well as a cat could smirk) at Luke. Luke narrowed his eyes and mouthed *you're dead* as he slid his thumb slowly across his throat, quickly dropping his hand and smiling widely when Emmie turned to face him. Dean chuckled lightly and Luke winked at him, the play fight forgotten, the easy brotherly camaraderie between them settling back in place.

-This portal will take us to a set of caves on the outskirts of one of the more populated villages. It's where I stayed when I was doing recon. They used to be deserted, but that was almost eight hundred years ago, so be ready.-

Emmie nodded and looked between the two of them.

"Are we ready, boys?"

THREE

"This is...my gods," Emmie whispered as they made their way cautiously through the village. The caves themselves were still deserted, just as they had been all those years ago when Dean had visited this realm, but now, so was the village. They'd watched from an outcropping of rock for a long time before venturing down into the town, but there had been no signs of life within. Not a soul wandered the streets, no sounds drifted upwards towards the caves, not a single twitch of movement from any window or doorway.

Now they saw why: there had been a massacre here.

Dean and Luke had both smelled the unmistakable stench of death before the trio walked through the broken gate leading into the village, and the fur along Dean's back stood up in alert and unease. Luke had glanced downward at him, their gazes locking and an unspoken agreement passing between them. It sent a strange thrill through Dean and an unexpected pang: it had been so long since he'd gone into battle beside someone, so long since that sense of trust shared among brothers in arms warmed his chest, an invisible chord connecting him with the man beside him. The fact that

Luke looked at him like a man now, despite his appearance, made Dean's throat feel tight.

Shaking himself, Dean tried to understand what could have happened here. This village had been inhabited by mostly harmless beings, with no riches to speak of and no power to be taken. Why would anyone attack them? Resources, perhaps? But then why not take them and leave the inhabitants alive? A killing spree made no real sense.

The attack had happened long enough ago that the blood had dried, leaving deep, brown stains against doorways and across cobblestones, but not so long that the bodies had crumbled to dust. A few weeks maybe, Dean thought as he lightly trailed down the wide dirt roadway through the village between Emmie and Luke. Luke had his swords out and at the ready, and while he was supremely skilled with almost every weapon you could think of, Dean knew that his most deadly weapon was *himself*.

If they were truly in danger, Luke would change into a lethal, terrifying, giant wolf. Dean liked to give him shit about his transformation, calling him pup and asking if he wanted to stick his head out the window as they drove through the streets near Luke's home, but Dean was honestly in awe of Luke in his wolf form. He'd seen Luke fight, both as a man and as a wolf, and the warrior in Dean had been impressed and fascinated with the way he moved, the lethal grace with which he dispatched his opponents no matter what form he was in.

Now, he longed to take one of the swords from Luke's hand, to stand beside him and fight like a man, like the man Luke seemed to see him as despite his admittedly adorable fuzzy paws and twitchy whiskers. He had an undeniable urge to protect both Luke and Emmie, something deep within his chest *demanding* that he do so, telling him it was his duty. But he could do little to protect either of them as a fucking cat. The need to find Sabina was riding him harder these last few weeks, harder than it ever had in the past five centuries. Of course, he'd been desperate to get back to his true form since the moment he was changed, but now it was different. It was a panicked kind of need, almost desperate, and he wasn't quite sure why. Sure, there was a foreboding in the air and Emmie had hinted that something big and bad was coming, and he knew he needed to be in his true form to be able to truly fight back against it, but it was more than that. It was something more personal, something that he felt deep in his soul.

They made their way through the entire village, finding nothing but bodies. Not all goblins, of course, though most were. Many other species had settled here as well when the mining deep in the mountains had begun, so the corpses were a mix of beings, none of which deserved these fates. Some were stabbed through the back, as if they'd been running for their lives. Others had wounds on their hands, as if they'd tried to shield themselves from the blows.

Dean swallowed back bile, rage flaring as his eyes roamed over the smaller, child-sized bodies. He could feel his power rise within his chest, like a fire slowly spreading through his veins, his blood heating and boiling. His curse prevented his power from actually manifesting, so it simply roiled around within him, burning and burning with impotent rage. *Fuck this fucking body.*

They continued to wind through the bodies, and Dean couldn't help but scrunch his nose at a particularly unsightly large goblin, though he knew it probably made him a fucker. Goblins were never attractive creatures, even on the best of days, but now, with their bodies crumbled and twisted in the agony of their last moments, their greenish skin now gray with death, they were truly grotesque. That was probably an unkind thing to say about the dead, but it was the truth.

"Ugly bastards," Luke muttered, echoing Dean's silent thoughts. Or, he was fairly sure they'd been silent. Sometimes, it was almost *too* easy to speak to Dean and Emmie, to put his words into their minds without even trying. He needed to guard his tongue—and mind—better, lest he share something he *really* shouldn't...because he had plenty of thoughts these days that should definitely remain private.

"They are that," Emmie agreed, though she looked distraught over all of the death surrounding them.

A scraping noise emanated from just inside the open doorway of a rickety old building that looked as if a slight breeze may blow the entire thing over. Luke immediately shifted to put Emmie and Dean behind him, but Dean quickly leapt forward to stand beside him.

-Nice try, pup-

"You're a fucking *cat*," Luke all but growled.

-And you're an overgrown mutt. I can hold my own, you fucker-

Luke rolled his eyes and let out an exasperated breath, but Dean thought he saw the corners of the man's lips twitch upward in amusement. The two of them stalked forward slowly.

"Is someone there?" Luke called.

"Haven't you ever watched a horror movie?" Emmie hissed. "You never ask '*is someone there?*' you idiot. That's like Scary Movie Survival 101!"

"Well then we're all going to die anyway since I know sure as shit none of us are virgins," Luke replied and Dean chuckled silently. Oh no, they were all far, *far* from that. Though, of course for him, it had been half a millennium since the last time he'd gotten laid...Dean quickly forced the thoughts away. It was near torture to think of sex, to imagine all of the things he longed for but couldn't have in this body...He shuddered and more forcefully kicked the thoughts out of his head. *Fucking focus, damn it.*

A small figure dragged itself forward out of the shadowed doorway on gnarled arms. Its legs were gone completely, though it looked as if that had always been the case, not as if it had happened in the attack. Luke raised his sword, but only half-heartedly. This creature obviously posed no threat.

Emmie darted forward and both Dean and Luke let out mild curses under their breath, following close on her heels.

"What happened here?" she asked gently as she neared the

goblin. It looked up at her with large, black eyes, the whites streaked with red. Dried blood was crusted below its bulbous nose and down its chin.

"The Order of Valen. They came...from the mountains," the goblin wheezed. "They never come. In the two hundred years I've lived, they've never...come here. They...stay away. Until now." He coughed violently, blood and spittle flying. "They demanded sacrifices...they said she was not herself...that they had not given her enough offerings." Another rattling cough. "We are not fighters... were not ready to defend..."

Its eyes slid closed and for a moment, Dean thought that the thing had passed on, but its lids slowly fluttered back open. Its big eyes were wet and glassy.

"They came and...they slaughtered everyone," it whispered. The cult had done this? Sacrifices? Not herself? *What in the fuck is going on?* Dean knew that most of the villagers were of a more docile species of goblin but larger, vicious varieties did exist, and now he thought that the cult was most likely full of the bastards judging by the carnage.

"All but you," Luke said, flatly. It came out cold and uncaring, but Dean knew that was just what he was showing on the surface. Luke had a reputation for being robotic when it came to emotions and feelings, but Dean already knew that was bullshit. That may be what he *wanted* everyone to think, but it was far from the truth.

"I...hid," the goblin admitted, breath hitching. His—Dean was fairly sure it was male now that he looked at the creature more closely—chest was rising and falling in disjointed heaves and Dean could tell he wasn't long for this world. "Could not run," he said, the ghost of a smile pulling his crusted lips upward, making the scabs crack and a new trickle of blood run down the side of his mouth, "obviously. My supplies ran out a week ago...dying now. *Finally,*" he added in an almost wistful sigh.

"Where are they? The Order?" Luke demanded, though his tone was a bit gentler this time.

"Through the...pass in the Black Mountain. The old mining compound..."

With that, he took one last heaving breath and then his chest stilled. His eyes glossed over, staring upward but seeing nothing.

Emmie stood, face pinched, but her runes rippled with silvery light.

"I would very much like to kill the Order of Valen please," she said. Emmie wasn't typically a violent being, per se, but she fought for what was right and for the people she loved with a brutality that was staggering. Hell, she'd given up being a Fate because of the love she had for her brother, in order to give him his chance at happiness. She was terrifyingly powerful and you did *not* want to be on the receiving end of it. Dean had seen her render entire armies to piles of charred bones in a matter of minutes.

Bottom line: don't get on Emmie's shit list.

-I second that-

"Motion fucking carried," Luke said, sheathing his swords with a satisfying *scnick* sound.

CHAPTER
FOUR

They camped in the caves for the night, deciding to make their way north at first light. Emmie wasn't used to having to huff it like a mortal, but they'd discovered soon after arriving that her phasing didn't work here. Some realms were like that, negating certain powers and abilities, and no one particularly knew why. Probably just a big joke by the Powers that Be to keep life interesting, she supposed. She could still phase out of the realm and back again now that she knew where it was, but all traveling within the realm had to be done in the good old-fashioned way of foot traffic.

And it sucked balls.

She was ready to find Sabina, kill the cultist, and get the fuck out of here as soon as possible.

Luke found a large, secure cavern and, after checking every nook and cranny, deemed it safe enough for the evening.

"Stay here with her," he told Dean quietly, "I'll be back." As if she couldn't take care of herself. She rolled her eyes, but part of her thought it was sweet that he felt the need to protect her. He left the cave and Dean came to poke his nose in the supplies as she began to unpack them.

-Are you alright, love?-

She nodded. "I am. There was just so much needless death..." She shook her head. "We're going to avenge that village, I'm sure of it. Well, not *completely* sure," she added, brows drawing down. "This realm is messing with my powers, even my foresight. I'm getting flashes, but I can't see everything with the usual clarity." She sighed and rubbed her temples. She was doing her best to hide it from her friends, but her visions were threatening to tear her mind apart lately. There were too many possibilities, too many outcomes ahead, and most of them weren't good. Darkness was coming. War. And death. Lots and lots of death.

So, she was taking matters into her own hands and steering things a bit more than was advisable. It had started decades ago, just little things here and there to get all of the pieces in the proper places on the cosmic chessboard, but now the game had really started. Things had worked out the way she needed them to with Hades and Skylar, and Beck and Poseidon were on their way, but so much was still changing, nothing was as solid as it should be.

She was steering, but she could only do so much. Already she was being punished from afar for her meddling, but she was gritting and bearing it, rubbing some dirt in it, as Skylar liked to say. But the visions often came with pain now, sharp, agonizing stabs of it. Not always, but sometimes, and it was enough to make her knees want to buckle. She would take the pain though. What was coming was too dangerous, too potentially devastating to leave it all up to chance. She would do whatever she had to in order to save the people she loved, save all of the worlds as they knew them.

-Do any of those flashes involve me not having a tail anymore by chance?- Dean asked, and she could hear the smirk in his voice inside her mind.

"Perhaps," she said cryptically, her own lips curling upward. She was...ninety percent sure this was going to finally be the answer for him. But she didn't want to fully believe it, not yet. She wanted Dean back in his true form so badly she could barely stand it. The vision of her reaching for him—*of reaching for him and Lucas*—never stopped playing in her mind. She needed to understand it, needed to know if what she believed it to mean could possibly be true.

After a few minutes, Dean's tail began swishing in agitation.

-Where is that fucking pup? It's been too long...-

Emmie's lips twitched. "Worried about him?"

-Of course I am. We're in a wasteland of a realm and a sadistic, bloodthirsty cult just wiped out an entire village!- His cat eyes narrowed at her.

"You care about him, don't you?"

-I...-

He didn't finish his thought. Luke came strolling back into the cave, arms loaded down with wood. His forehead was beaded with sweat, his damp shirt clinging to his muscles in a way that made Emmie's stomach clench and her mouth water. He dropped the wood into a pile, straightening and shaking his brownish-blonde hair off of his brow in a very wolfy way. He normally kept it shorter, more of a clean-cut-military style, and he rocked that look like nobody's business, but the slightly longer look made him positively devastating. It was just long enough on the top to look tousled when he ran his hands through it, and that, combined with his thick scruff gave him a rugged and dangerous look that was beyond sexy.

He wiped his hands on his tactical pants, the dark fabric hugging his muscular legs. He paused and tilted his head at Emmie and Dean.

"What?"

Emmie shook herself, realizing that both she and Dean were staring at him. Ok, gawking really. Ogling. Maybe drooling...If Dean wasn't a cat, she was sure they'd be wearing matching expressions of admiration and...hunger. *Gods, the things I want to do to that body...*

-We were starting to wonder if you'd gotten distracted chasing your tail, pup- Dean said to them both.

"Hilarious. Really. I had to chop wood," he said, a bit defensively. He would never admit it, but Emmie knew that being around a demigod and a...whatever she was—even she truly didn't know what to call herself anymore. A "godly being" was about as close as anything she guessed—made Luke feel inadequate. He was one of the strongest supernatural beings Emmie had ever seen, aside from Dalton Pembroke and one particularly ruthless dragon shifter she'd encountered centuries ago, but even still, she could understand why he felt...less than. He'd only recently even learned that the gods truly existed. Now, he was surrounded by them almost constantly, seeing their great displays of power and strength. That would be enough for even the mightiest of the mighty to have moments of doubt.

"Well, go ahead and channel your inner caveman and make fire, I'm freezing."

Though the day had been near sweltering, once the rust-colored sun had set behind Black Mountain in the distance, the temperature had dropped drastically. Lucas did as ordered and she tried and failed not to stare as he knelt beside the small pit they'd made out of stones from around the cave. He quickly coaxed flames to life and the fire highlighted his hazel eyes, more golden brown than green tonight, his strong jaw, the faint scar running through his right eyebrow.

She sighed inwardly. Lucas McBride may not be a god, but he was sure built like one.

They ate dinner around the fire and strategized a plan for getting to the Order. Dean estimated it would take them two or three days to get to the foot of the mountains, but once there, they could rest and do recon before heading through the pass and breaching the compound.

-*Centuries ago, they mined gemstones from within Black Mountain, it's why that compound even exists. The last time I was here, it was inhabited by miners and overseers and traders. Now apparently the Order has moved in and hung the* Cult Sweet Cult *sign on the door. We should be able to get a good vantage point to scout from these hills here-* He indicated to the map they'd scrawled into the dirt floor of the cave, pointing his nose towards the area surrounding the mountain itself.

Luke nodded, eyes serious as he studied the map, and Emmie

could see the wheels turning, working through possibilities and plans, back up plans and back up plans to the back up plans. Like Skylar, he'd been trained by Skylar's adoptive father, Dalton, and he had one of the most impressive strategic minds Emmie had ever seen. He rivaled even Ares and that was truly saying something. A funny twist of fate that Skylar's biological father and her adoptive one were both born warriors and war strategists. Skylar was ready to wring Emmie's neck for keeping the whereabouts of Dalton a secret —and Luke wasn't too happy about it either—but it was all necessary. *Sometimes you gotta be cruel to be kind.*

"That's a good plan. Do you know anything about the inside of the compound? Layout or where they may be keeping her?" Luke asked.

Dean shook his head. *-Not really, no. I captured the bounty just before he made it through the pass, so I spied it from afar, but didn't go inside.-*

Emmie hid a wince as a vision flashed in her mind, feeling like a hot blade was being shoved into her temple.

"She's underground. In a cell or dungeon..." She closed her eyes, focusing on the hazy flashes, forcing them to slow so she could pick out more details. The sooner she got out of this realm, the better. She wasn't used to having to put so much effort into seeing things, and she was over it already. Not just because it was annoying, but because there was too much at stake right now for her to not be at the top of her game. A thousand possible futures lay ahead, and she needed everything to happen just right in order for the *one* where they were victorious to come to pass.

"There's...running water somewhere nearby. Splashes. A stream or a fountain maybe?" And then the vision was gone.

Luke nodded. "Good. That's good. We'll be able to get a general location once we do some scouting. We should try to get some rest." They spread the two bedrolls near each other, and Emmie and Luke's gazes met. Had they both just realized at the same moment that they would be sleeping mere feet away from each other tonight? She'd slept at his place more than once over the past few months, but this felt entirely different than crashing in his spare bedroom or passing out on one of the couches in the living room.

Luke's eyes darkened to a deep amber and his hands balled into fists at his sides. Something thick settled in the air, something dangerous and combustible...something Emmie needed more than her next breath.

Luke cleared his throat. "I'll take first watch—"

-*I'll do it*- Dean cut in. There was something in his voice. Not jealousy exactly, and not quite pain, but something close to both. Before Luke could argue, Dean nimbly bolted from the cavern, leaving the two of them alone.

CHAPTER

FIVE

This was bad.

Or very, very good.

Luke and Emmie had been skating around the tension between them for weeks. It was palpable almost anytime they were around each other, a barely contained fire that threatened to burn out of control if one tiny spark found the kindling. They'd flirted and done some dirty texting, but nothing physical had happened yet. They'd come very close a couple of weeks ago, in his apartment. She'd been sitting on the kitchen counter, having hopped up there when he went into his office to look through some text or another. As soon as he'd walked back in the room, their eyes had locked, just like they had a moment ago before Dean left the cavern, and the air had practically sparked around them with electricity.

He'd walked to her without a word, her eyes widening and the lavender ring flaring brightly around her darkening violet irises. She'd automatically spread her knees when he'd reached the counter in front of her and he'd settled himself between her thighs. He'd placed his palms on either side of her ass on the counter and waited, barely keeping control, barely holding himself still. She ran her hands up his chest, eyes sliding closed as he leaned forward. He still didn't kiss her, but lightly ran his nose along hers, putting their lips so close together that her soft gasps felt *almost* like a kiss, so close that their breaths mingled, that her heat consumed him.

"Emmie," he breathed, fingers clenching and digging into the counter. Her own fingers curled into his shirt and she shifted her hips ever so slightly forward, enough that she pressed against him and he barely bit back a moan.

"Luke," she whispered. "Gods I want you...but...we're about to be interrupted," she sighed. Sure enough, a few seconds later Skylar and Hades had appeared for an impromptu movie night. As much as Luke loved seeing them—well, Skylar anyway. He was still getting used to the fact that the actual God of the fucking Underworld existed. Being comfortable hanging out and playing Xbox together was going to take a bit more time—he'd wanted nothing more in that moment than to toss them both out on their asses and carry Emmie to his room like a caveman.

Similar things happened more than once. They would be seconds away from finally doing something and she would see an interruption. She said it was the Powers That Be—whoever the hell that was—fucking with her to prove a point, but he wasn't sure if she was serious or not.

He braced himself now, waiting for the news that an interruption was coming, that he couldn't have her. They stared at each other, the tension growing by the second, the cave suddenly feeling anything but cold. He wasn't sure that he could keep himself from touching her now, from kissing her like his life fucking depended on it, no matter what she was about to tell him. He knew he had about thirty more seconds of self-control before he snapped.

"Emmie, I—"

He didn't have time to finish his sentence. She threw herself at him, wrapping her arms around the back of his neck and slamming her lips to his. He froze for the briefest of moments, surprise and relief washing over him, but then his arms went around her, pulling her close. Her lips were soft and warm against his, just as he imagined they'd be. And *fuck* had he imagined.

He sucked lightly on her bottom lip, making her moan, and then his tongue was thrusting against hers and her fingers were digging into the back of his head, tangling in his hair, pulling him even harder against her. She pressed him backwards, following him as they moved until his back hit the stone. He quickly turned so that she was against the wall, and pressed himself hard against her, covering her body with his.

She gasped loudly, and his cock pulsed, desperate. He shifted his hips against her again and her gasp turned into a low moan. *God—er, god*s, *plural*, he silently corrected himself. Would he ever get used to that?

"Luke," she whispered in a choked voice. He ran his hands up her sides, slipping them beneath her t-shirt, and skated his fingers across her bare skin. So soft. So warm. He yanked the shirt up, pulling it over her head. He stared down after tossing the shirt away. She wore a white, lace bra that stood out against her beautiful brown skin, the silver tattoos shimmering brightly in the dim light of the cave. Her chest heaved with her panting breaths, and he wanted nothing more than to kiss and lick every inch of her. He leaned in to kiss her again, lifting her up and urging her legs around his waist. She locked her ankles around his lower back and he turned, walking them back towards the blankets.

He dropped to his knees and gently laid her back, following her down and settling his body over hers. She gasped and dug her fingers into his back as he kissed across her jaw and down her throat, nipping lightly as he went. When he got to the spot where her neck met her shoulder, he nearly growled, his instincts flaring and demanding that he mark her there. It was the way of wolf shifters and full-blooded lupines alike to mark their mates with a bite the first time they were claimed. *So, she's truly mine then?* he thought, a little dazed. Yes, there was no denying that his instincts were telling him that she was, and yet...there was still something off, something missing.

He forced himself to continue on, knowing that this was not the time or place to claim her. He trailed kisses down her chest, over the swells of her breasts.

"Luke," she groaned, nearly begging, fingers laced in his hair. He quickly unlatched the clasp between her breasts, and suddenly forgot how to breathe. *Perfect. So fucking perfect.* He palmed her breasts, and her back bowed, pressing them harder into his hands. He leaned down, using his grip to direct one jutting nipple to his mouth. He closed his lips over the peak and she gasped loudly, hips arching upward and her runes flashing brightly. "Oh *gods.*"

Luke groaned around her nipple, sucking gently before twirling his tongue, then sucking harder. Her hips writhed beneath him and he reluctantly released his prize, only to shift to the other side and continue his torture. Gods she was beautiful, every inch of her perfectly made. She yanked his head upward again, slamming her lips to his once more, tongue thrusting hard against his. He could see the flaring light of her tattoos behind his closed lids, like tiny fireworks.

He shifted so he was lying beside her and ran one palm downward over her stomach. He stopped when the tips of his fingers dipped just below the waistband of her shorts.

"I need you to tell me to stop if...if I need to stop," he managed to say against her lips. If he moved his hand down another two inches, he was done for. Then, out of nowhere, Dean's face flashed behind his eyes, though it wasn't a cat's face, it was a man's. Of course, Luke had no idea what Dean truly looked like—when he'd asked, the smartass had only replied with *"Adonis looks like Quasimodo compared to me, pup"*— but he supposed he'd simply conjured an image in his head based on what he thought Dean would look like. But the question was, *why* was he thinking about Dean right now? He shook himself as the answer worked its way through the lust-fog covering his brain.

"I mean, I know..." He took a settling breath. He couldn't deny what was plain to see, regardless of his feelings. "I know that you have feelings for Dean, too, so if you don't want to...I mean, if you don't want *us* to..." He shook his head in frustration. He was usually much smoother than this.

"Don't stop," she breathed in answer, leaning up to gently bite at his lower lip. His entire body shuddered, and suddenly all thoughts about anything else outside of this moment and the two of them and the feel of her body beneath his disappeared. He shoved his hand downward, wedging it beneath the fabric of her shorts. He didn't have much wiggle room with them being so damned tight—not that he was complaining: he'd appreciated the view of her ass in the things as they'd hiked to the cave earlier—but it was hard to maneuver his big hand where it needed to be to, but—

"Fuck!" Emmie yelled when he pressed a finger inside her. *Godssss.* She was tight around his finger and so slick he had to clench his teeth against the instincts flaring inside him, demanding that he bury his cock deep inside her, that he bite her neck and claim her as his forever. *No, no, no. Not yet.* He couldn't figure out what was off and the claiming of a mate was a big thing. He didn't want to force it until he understood what was going on. After all of this was done, he'd talk to some of his shifter friends, see if they had ever experienced anything like this before. So, no, he wouldn't give her the claiming mark tonight, but that didn't mean he wasn't going to enjoy the hell out of himself.

She bucked and writhed as he thrust his finger, driving them both wild, and soon enough, he couldn't take it anymore. Lucas kissed down her body, licking and nipping and worshiping as he went before finally kneeling between her legs. He yanked her belt off, the buckle clinking loudly as it slammed into the stone wall. He yanked at the edges of her shorts, sliding them down her thighs and tossing them over his shoulder. Their gazes locked for a brief moment as he gripped the sides of her panties, and she bit her lip. The purple of her eyes had darkened to nearly black, the ring of lavender almost glowing now in its brightness against the deeper color.

"Yes?" he managed to ask, voice low and rough.

"*Yes*," she begged.

Luke nearly shuddered in relief and anticipation, not quite believing that this was finally happening. He tugged her panties down and sat back on his heels. He swallowed hard as Emmie let her knees fall wide, unashamed and unabashed and sexy as fucking hell. He scrubbed a hand over his mouth as he stared at her: wet and open and needy—*for him*. He knew she could have anyone she wanted, knew that she was *choosing* him and it made him want to beat his chest with stupid male pride.

He settled back between her thighs and didn't hesitate to dip his head, giving her pussy one long, slow lick. He made some unintelligible, animalistic sound deep in his chest at the taste of her and she cried out, back and hips arching off the ground. Gods, he was in heaven. The feel of her on his tongue, the sounds of her breathy moans in his ears, the taste of her...it was all too much and not nearly fucking enough. He'd never get enough of her, even if he lived forever, he'd never, ever have his fill.

She dug her hands into his hair, nails scraping along his scalp and making a shiver of pleasure skate down his spine. She panted his name over and over, almost like a prayer, as she writhed her hips, demanding more and more and more.

"Mmmm, so greedy, Em," he murmured with a grin.

"Feels. So. *Good*, Luke," she moaned, rocking her hips up to his mouth again. He gave her what she wanted—what she fucking needed—and thrust two fingers inside her as he sucked on her clit. She cried out in some language he had no hope of understanding and wind began to swirl around them inside the cave. She bucked wildly, breaths coming out in short, choppy bursts.

"That's it, baby. Come for me," he rasped and she whimpered. He flicked his tongue over her clit again before sucking hard.

"Luke, oh gods. Ohgodsohgodsohgods!"

Her tattoos flared even brighter, nearly blinding as she came in a rush. He felt her clenching his fingers, pulsing tightly over and over as her orgasm washed through her like a tidal wave. He quickly removed them, wanting her to finish coming on his tongue. He spread her wide and thrust his tongue deep inside, taking everything she had to give. Her moans echoed off of the rocks around them, the most perfect chorus of pleasure in his ears.

Later, he would feel a twinge of guilt knowing that Dean would have heard all of it from his perch outside. Later, thoughts he wouldn't understand would come flooding in. Later, he would need a stiff drink to try to muddle through it all and try to figure out what the fuck it all meant.

But for now, all Luke could focus on was the feel and taste of Emmie as she came apart from his touch. He wanted to do this all night, would if she let him, but she sat upright, yanking his head upward at the same time, surprising him with her swiftness and strength. He *knew* she was strong, but her delicate frame made it easy to forget sometimes. She pulled his lips to hers, kissing him hard and deep and languidly. If she minded tasting herself on his tongue, she didn't show it, and fuck was it hot. She trailed her hand downward and quickly palmed his painfully hard cock through his pants, making him groan.

"Let's do something about this, shall we?" she whispered against his lips, and he could feel her grin. She dipped her fingers under the waistband of his pants, brushing the swollen crown, and he hissed in a breath between clenched teeth. Fuck, even the slightest touch had him feeling like he was on fire. She made an appreciative hum and within a heartbeat, his belt was somehow unbuckled, his fly open, and her hand wrapped around his cock.

"Fuckkkk," he groaned into her neck, nipping gently as his hands tightened in her hair. Her head lolled back and he kissed along the column of her neck, her pulse racing beneath his tongue as she stroked, over and over. Her hands on him felt so good, so right. How had he survived this long without her? Without this feeling of connection? She swiped her thumb over the slit and spread the bead of moisture over the head and he bucked his hips harder into her grasp. Gods, he was going to fucking explode.

"Lucas," she whispered hoarsely, "I want to know how you taste."

All thought left his brain and he jerked upright, meeting her gaze. He wanted to say something—*you don't have to,* or *please for the love of all the gods, don't be kidding,* maybe, but he couldn't quite form any words at all. He'd never wanted anything so badly in his life and he swallowed hard as she held his gaze. She smiled knowingly and he gasped her name quietly as she started kissing her way down his neck, flicking her tongue and grazing her teeth along his skin in a way that made his eyes roll back in his head. But then Dean's voice treaded quietly into their minds.

-Sorry to interrupt but...you need to see this- His voice belied no hint of anger or jealousy, though it did seem a little strained.

"Damn it," Emmie said, frustration clear in her voice, and she reluctantly released his cock. Luke gnashed his teeth, jaw clenching tightly as he tried to get a hold on himself. He called on all of his years of training, the decades of punishing workouts and exercises and drills that he'd put himself through to master every physical aspect of his body. He closed his eyes and took deliberate, controlled breaths until his heart rate slowed and his thoughts cleared. They both stood and got themselves put to rights and then Emmie leaned her forehead against his chest.

"Didn't see that coming," she sighed "I'm sorry."

Luke gently pushed her shoulders, putting a bit of space between them and urging her to look up at him. He put one finger under her chin, tilting it up so that she met his gaze fully.

"Nothing to apologize for, Em. I am perfectly content to be left hanging," he said with a crooked smile, and she huffed out a soft laugh. He leaned down and kissed her gently and she wrapped her arms around his neck. After a few minutes she pulled away and grinned.

"I've been waiting eons for that, you know—*literally.*"

Luke huffed out a laugh. He would wait forever to be with Emmie —but dear gods he hoped he wouldn't have to. He twirled a lock of silver hair between his fingers before tucking it behind her ear. He sighed, kissed her once more, and tugged her towards the tunnel leading out into the night.

CHAPTER

SIX

For the first time in centuries, Dean didn't know what he felt. He'd accepted long ago that everyone around him would go on with their lives while he was stuck in this form, and he'd never begrudged them for it, not a single time. Of course, he wished it had been *him* with Emmie all these years, but he'd been happy that she'd found solace and companionship with others. Hell, he even secretly loved when she'd recount her role playing with Charon over breakfast to a hilariously disgruntled Hades. It was hot as hell imagining the two of them playing a little *Outlander* together—the big ferryman of the Underworld really did bear a striking resemblance to Jamie Fraser.

So, yes, he loved her enough to want all of that for her, even without him. She deserved to be happy. She deserved *everything*. So, why was his chest burning now with...he didn't even know what. Jealousy, hurt, envy, longing, bitterness, resentment...the list was too long and the emotions were all swirling up together in a way that made him want to bellow to the stars. He'd known for weeks now how Luke felt about Emmie. It was obvious for anyone to see. And Emmie loved him back.

Dean knew that she still loved him too, but no one could deny that a part of her heart had been given to Lucas. He should be happy for her, shouldn't he, for both of them? And he was, on some level, he really was, but he also very much...wasn't. Why? What was so different this time?

Dean sighed, knowing the answer. It was different this time, because now, it wasn't *just* Emmie. Now, there was Lucas as well. There was no use in denying it anymore: Dean had somehow managed to fall in love with both of them, his heart split right down the fucking middle. He knew that Luke had already come to regard him as a close friend, seemed to have a deep connection with him that made Dean wonder...but no, Luke would likely never feel *that* way about him. It was just wishful thinking. As far as he knew, Luke had only ever been attracted to or in relationships with females. *Plus, he can't possibly even think about having feelings for a fucking cat.*

Dean's claws flared out in frustration and he longed to dig them into Sabina's pretty face, use them to rip out her flaming red hair until the strands darkened with blood. He tried to calm himself, but the last few minutes kept replaying in his mind: the unmistakable sounds of clothes being shed, of lips being kissed and skin being scratched, and the scent of lust and pleasure filling the air. For the first time, Dean cursed his enhanced senses, remembering how their breaths came faster and harsher as he imagined they became more frenzied and desperate, how Luke had groaned and growled, nearly animalistic in his need, how Emmie whimpered and gasped and cried out as she came, how the scent of her had filled his senses and made him nearly crazed. His power roiled inside him, desperate and useless.

Dean squeezed his eyes shut now. Sure, he'd been jealous—and he wasn't even sure which one he was more jealous of, Emmie or Luke—but he'd also been insanely aroused by it all. Hearing them, smelling them, picturing them...

Fuck, is that creepy? That's probably creepy.

What the fuck was it that mortals said when they needed to

otherwise occupy their minds in sexual situations? Think of base-ball? So, Dean tried to recall every baseball statistic he'd ever read over the past hundred years while he waited for the two to emerge from the cave. He felt slightly more settled when they finally came out, a bit disheveled.

Emmie looked more relaxed than she had in weeks and Dean felt a pang in his chest. He knew that the strain of trying to steer the outcome of the future was heavy on her shoulders and wished there was something more he could do to help. Hopefully, once they found Sabina and lifted this fucking curse, he could find a way to ease her burden somehow.

Dean regarded them both with steady eyes as they approached, and to his surprise, Luke's cheeks flushed and he rubbed the back of his neck a little self-consciously. It was...cute. Fucking adorable actually.

Fuck, fuck, fuck.

"What's going on?" Emmie asked, wrapping her arms around herself as a cold wind blew across the small outcropping of rocks in front of the cave.

Lucas moved to stand beside Dean, who leapt up onto a boulder, putting them closer in height. Dean hated being at ground level and having to stare up at everyone all the time. He tilted his head and managed to convey a smirk through his feline face.

-Be careful with that, pup. You'll poke someone's eye out- He very pointedly cut his eyes to Luke's crotch where his hardon had yet to completely vanish. *Good gods.* Even only half hard, his bulge was... impressive. *Gulp. Yum. Help.*

"Fuck off," Luke huffed through gritted teeth, but his cheeks reddened again. Was Luke...*shy*? Surely not. Was it just because it was coming from a man and he wasn't comfortable with that? Dean studied his friend and Luke met his gaze. Even in the darkness, Dean could make out the bright green flecks against the golden brown. His gaze was steady, and...*something* flashing behind his eyes, though it was gone so quickly Dean couldn't quite pinpoint what it was.

Disappointment maybe? Or something close to it? Whatever it was, it didn't appear to be a sense of discomfort. As if Dean couldn't be more intrigued by the boy, now there was a new layer to unravel. Deciding to let it lie for the time being, Dean jerked his head to the west where a line of floating lights bobbed along like stars on the dark horizon.

-Look there-

Luke squinted and frowned. "Is that a caravan?"

-It is. Looks like they're bringing some sacrifices back home with too. Probably hit one of the smaller villages too.-

Though the caravan was far off in the distance, slowly making its way across the scorched desert that laid between them and Black Mountain, Dean could see the wagons with bars on the windows, could hear the chains rattling and the quiet crying of the beings within.

"Fuck," Luke grunted.

Emmie's tattoos flared and silvery light seemed to hover just above the surface of her skin, like an aurora. Dean knew exactly what she was thinking, and knew how angry she was that she couldn't actually do anything about it.

"I can't wait to kill these bastards," she gritted.

Luke laid a hand on Emmie's shoulder. Gods how Dean longed to be able to do the same, to comfort those that he loved in that way. Sure, kitten cuddles were nice, but it wasn't the fucking same. She sighed, shoulders slumping. The light dimmed around her and her runes faded back to a light, shimmering silver.

"We'll make it right," Luke promised.

-Which of course means we'll kill the bastards slowly- Dean added. She gave them both half-smiles.

"I'm going to bed," she said quietly, turning to walk back into the cave, running a hand through her long, slightly-tangled silver hair.

The two men (so-to-speak) stood together watching the lights of the caravan slowly make their way over the gray sand, now black as pitch under the night sky.

"Hey, are you...I mean, with me and Emmie...I know..." Luke let out a long exhale and ran a hand through his hair before crossing his arms over his massive chest. "Are *we* alright?" he asked. Dean stared, surprised that Luke would be worried about that, and he did sound truly worried. *Fuck.* If Dean hadn't already known he was falling in love with the fucking wolf, this may have crystallized things. The guy just hooked up with someone who was as close to a goddess as you could get without actually being one, and he was wasting his time being worried if his friendship with Dean was on solid ground.

-*Of course we are*- When Luke arched a skeptical brow, Dean continued -*Everyone knows that I've been in love with her for centuries upon centuries. But, for now, there's nothing I can do about those feelings. You* can *do something about yours and I wouldn't dare try to stop you or be upset about that. I...care about both of you enough to want you both happy. Am I jealous? Sure. But not in a way that would make me angry at either of you.*-

"Is it that obvious, then? How I feel about..." Lucas' gaze met Dean's and he quickly cleared his throat, "how I feel?" he finished. Luke sighed but there was an hard edge to it and he seemed tense. Was he really worried about anyone knowing how he felt about Emmie? Why would he be?

Dean chuckled, wanting to ease the wolf.

-*Probably not to everyone, but I've come to know you pretty well, pup*-

"You'd tell me if you weren't good with this, right? If it bothered you?"

Dean studied him.

-*And if I said it did? Would you end things with her? Could you do that?*-

"I..." Luke's pulse sped up and real panic flashed in his eyes.

-*Calm down, Lucas. I'm just fucking around. If it bothered me, that would* be *my issue, not yours. I wouldn't ask you to choose...And I'd never ask her to choose either*- he added.

Luke let out a long exhale and their gazes met again, holding for a long moment. Lucas' lips parted as if he wanted to say something, but he pressed them into a hard line and pushed himself off the boulder.

"I better head back inside and get a couple of hours sleep before my shift."

-Go chase all the dream rabbits your wolfy little heart desires-

"Don't make me get the laser pointer."

Dean chuffed quietly in laughter and watched the entrance to the cave long after Luke had disappeared into the shadows.

I am in deep shit.

CHAPTER
SEVEN

"Why do mortals do this for *recreation*??" Emmie griped as they trudged through the seemingly endless charred wasteland leading to Black Mountain. "This is torture. Actually, scratch that. I was tortured twice, and both times were *way* more fun than this. Zero out of Ten; do not recommend."

-Has anyone ever told you that you're a touch dramatic, love?-

She threw a rock at the cat and he lithely skittered out of the way.

"Is it break time? I feel like it should be break time." Her feet were already throbbing and they still had at least five more hours until it was time to stop for the night. They were passing what looked like it may have been a building of some sort once upon a time, a small outpost on the way to the mining compound maybe? But now it was two half-walls forming a right angle and piles of crumbling stones. Luke eyed the rubble and stopped, the others following suit.

"You can rest here. I'm going to change and scout ahead."

"You need to rest too, you know," Emmie pointed out. Though they hadn't done anything else physically taxing during the night, she knew he hadn't slept much during the few hours he laid beside her, arms wrapped tightly around her, his chest rising and falling steadily against her back. Then it had been his turn on watch and he'd left her alone beneath the covers. Dean had curled up beside her for the rest of the night, and she'd fallen asleep stroking his soft fur. She could admit she was going to miss that a tiny bit once they lifted this pesky curse.

Speaking of pesky curses, Poseidon was soon going to learn about a doozy he himself had been saddled with without ever even knowing it. *But, so long as things go the way I want them to, all will be well soon...*

Luke leaned toward her, about to kiss her goodbye, but then seemed to think better of it, straightening again and simply running his hand down her arm instead. She knew that he'd been worried about Dean after last night, about how their relationship may affect him, and it made her heart clench to know that the two of them were already so close.

She chewed on her lip as she looked between them. Was it possible to love them each equally? Because she was fairly certain that she did. They were like two separate pieces of her soul, as if it had been split into thirds long, long ago and only now had all of the pieces found their way back together.

But will I have to choose in the end?

She...had no idea. She'd had flashes of visions of each of them with her, two separate futures, but it didn't *feel* like two distinct outcomes as visions often did. Usually it was plain that *Future A* was what happened if a certain choice was made, and *Future B* was what happened if a different one was. They were separate and distinct.

But her futures with Dean and Luke didn't feel that way, they felt as if they overlapped somehow. It was strange and she wasn't quite sure what to make of it. She'd asked Allister if he'd ever experienced such a thing, and though he hadn't, he'd had a perfectly plausible explanation for it. One she didn't let herself believe, not yet.

But when she thought about having to choose between them, her chest literally ached, a pain like hot knives slicing through her heart. So, she didn't think about it. Not yet. She wasn't used to having to wait and see, to figure things out as they came, and she had to say, she wasn't a fan. *How do normal people deal with this??* She liked knowing almost everything. Sure, it was a lot to shoulder and sometimes it was painful, but overall, eons of knowing what was to come was really fucking stupendous. Did people still say stupendous? Sometimes she got mixed up on when she was in the grand scheme of the universe's timeline. If it wasn't still popular, it should be. It was a stupendous word.

Luke gave them both a hard nod and in the span of a heartbeat, he changed. Gone was the six-foot-tall slab of muscle with a chiseled jaw and penetrating gaze. Now, a hulking, monstrous wolf stood before them. Deep gray fur, nearly as a large as a horse, with claws as long as Emmie's entire hand. He was fearsome and lethal and...ok, weirdly sexy. *Don't ask me to explain it.*

-Be safe, pup-

Luke rolled his eyes, now completely golden in his wolf form. Dean's eyes shifted to full gold with emotion as well, but his roiled like liquified metal. Luke's were like polished bits of golden amber. Both beautiful. A flash of both pairs of golden eyes staring up at her as they knelt before her, unmistakable hunger in their gazes, slammed into her mind, making her inhale sharply, and then it was gone, drifting away like smoke and she couldn't even clearly remember what it had been. They both tilted their heads at her but she waved them off, telling them she was alright, though she was rattled by the vision. Rattled and...turned on. Had...had they been doing what she *thought* they were doing? Or about to do it anyway? No, that couldn't be right...

-Be back soon- Luke said to each of them telepathically. Shifters could speak telepathically in their animal forms with anyone they chose. It was something that gave them an advantage during battle, and was very handy when you needed information form a wolf or a panther or whatever the hell the animal in question was.

He bounded away, eerily silent and graceful despite his hulking form.

-Is it weird that it's sexy when he does that? That's probably weird, right?-

Emmie laughed and dug around in her pack for her water bottle. She drank a few sips and poured some into a small bowl for Dean. He'd long ago gotten over his initial humiliation of Emmie taking care of him like he was a pet, but now, he seemed rigid as he stalked along the crumbling stone wall and lowered his head to the water. *Wonder what that's about?*

"Are you alright? With what happened last night?" she asked, eyeing him intently. They had known and loved each other long enough not to skirt around anything.

-Yes and no- he answered honestly. She nodded in understanding and let it be for now. *-Have you seen anything else about what's coming?-*

A rush of heat coursed through her remembering that last flash, but she locked that away and cleared her throat lightly.

"A few flashes. I keep seeing Sabina chained in that dungeon-type place, but then I see us somewhere else, searching for...something. I can't tell what. We do find her, but we aren't done yet, though I can't tell you why." Emmie shook her head in frustration. "I don't know if it's this realm or the fact that I'm trying to see futures that are too closely tied to my own or what, but things aren't coming clearly."

-We'll figure it out, love. It's alright-

She flashed him a smile and then said in a low voice, laced with thinly-veiled desire, "I saw *us*, though..."

Dean straightened at that, seeming to have stopped breathing all together.

-Us...?-

"You and me...with you very much no longer a cat." She swallowed hard remembering the wisps of visions she'd gotten a few days ago: Dean's lips crashing to hers, sweat-slicked bodies writhing, bloody scratches down a bare back...She barely stopped a shudder. Despite her amazing night with Luke, coming hard on his tongue and wanting to go for another round with him as soon as humanly possible, she was also desperate for her vision of Dean to come to fruition. She loved them both, *needed* them both in a way she couldn't even fully comprehend or explain, even to herself.

She knew it wasn't fair for her to ask that they be ok with her being with each of them in turn, but she had been waiting a long, long, *long* time for this, for her chance at happiness and love, and she was going to take it. She'd spent thousands upon thousands of years using her powers to help others. Now, it was her turn.

In the words of David Rose: *it's my turn to take a selfish.*

-So...so we succeed then?? I'm going to be back to myself?-

"We do and you will. I can't pinpoint the exact time, whether it be tomorrow or a week from now, but it happens here, in this realm, I'm sure of it."

His yellow eyes watered and his small chest rose and fell heavily.

-It doesn't feel real. I suppose it won't until I'm no longer furry- They both chuckled. *-All thanks to Luke. If he hadn't found that text...-*

"We'll both owe him much," she agreed.

-You love him- It wasn't a question.

"Yes," Emmie told him honestly. Dean looked thoughtful, but not upset, and she studied him, still able to get a glimpse of the man behind his false form. She still knew him better than almost anyone else. "And you do too, don't you?" she added.

Dean exhaled roughly.

-It's...complicated-

"That is the lamest answer I've ever heard. All of you boys and your 'it's complicated,'" she said in a low, mocking voice, "I swear I'm going to wring all of your necks!"

He chuckled as much as a cat could chuckle.

-Once I'm back in my body, you can do whatever you like to me, love-

"Oh! Speaking of enchantments and curses, there's something I need to do!"

-We weren't precisely talking of either of those things, but...ok?-

"Be right back!" Before Dean could say anything in return, she disappeared, phasing to the falls not far from Poseidon's palace where the girls liked to hang out. As she knew they would be, Skylar, Beck, Lily, and Medusa were swimming and sunning themselves, discussing how Beck was falling for the sinfully sexy God of the Sea. The poor girl didn't realize how obvious it was. *Adorable*.

"Enchantments are tricky, aren't they?" Emmie asked airily, making everyone scream with her sudden arrival. Skylar immediately shoved Beck behind her and an instant later, a sword with golden flames etched along the blade was firmly in her grasp, matching flames flicking through her blonde and red hair. Emmie grinned, knowing exactly why Skylar was protecting Beck so fiercely and knowing exactly how annoying it was to Beck.

"What the fuck, Emmie!? You're supposed to be off on a grand old adventure with Dean and Lucas, like going full on Frodo Baggins right now!" Skylar snapped, her eyes burning with irritation. *Literally* burning: her pupils were twin flickering tongues of fire. She'd probably just managed to keep her magnificent phoenix wings from popping out, which was honestly a shame. Skylar in her full phoenix form was beautiful. And hot. And terrifying. All the things, really.

"We are and having a smashing time of it, thanks for asking." *Except hiking is seriously for the birds*, Emmie thought. "But I just wanted to pop in and say hi, and tell Lily that she's going to have to call a truce with her sister. We're all going to be fighting on the same side soon and we need all hands and claws and wings on deck. Soooo, good luck with that! Kloveyoubye!" Emmie blew a kiss and disappeared, the protests of her friends echoing in her ears as she phased away, grinning.

-*What was that about?*- Dean asked when she reappeared.

"Just had to deliver a little message." Dean shook his head and somehow managed a shrug, even in a cat's body. He'd known her long enough to just roll with the strange and confusing punches. His eyes slitted and glittered, and the voice inside her mind was practically a purr.

-*So...want to tell me any more about this vision of us you saw...?*-

~

THEY WALKED and walked and walked. Then, just for a change of pace, they walked some more. Emmie grumbled, but she slowly got used to the trekking. The desert was hard, packed dirt, so at least it was easy to walk on, but wicked wind storms blew up out of nowhere every so often, making the three of them duck behind the sparse twig-like excuses for trees that dotted the scorched earth for cover. They did exactly fuck all to shield them. Thankfully, they all had enhanced healing abilities and the cuts and abrasions left by the flying sand didn't last too long. It still didn't feel good though, and Emmie was starting to hate this realm more and more by the second.

"Oh thank all the fucking gods," Emmie breathed as they finally made it to the edge of the thick forest that stood between the desert and the mountain. The trees here were thick and gnarled, black with blood-red leaves. Emmie supposed they should look sinister, but she actually thought they were kind of beautiful—in an admittedly macabre kind of way, of course.

"Tim Burton would probably love this place," she mused, making Luke laugh.

"We'll get a little deeper into the woods—"

"Into the woods to grandmother's house!" Emmie sang, momentarily transforming into a small, black-haired girl with a red riding cloak and a basket full of bread and pastries.

Lucas closed his eyes are if praying for patience, but his lips curled up in amusement. "—and find a good place to camp for the night," he finished, wiping sweat from his brow. Emmie tried and failed to ignore the way his shirt clung to his broad chest, the way a rivulet of sweat trickled slowly down his temple, across his jaw, then running down his throat. She swallowed hard but forced herself to focus. Mostly.

"Don't act like you didn't enjoy watching *Into the Woods* with me, Lucas McBride. I've heard you humming *Any Moment* more than once."

-I've heard you singing *it in the shower, actually-*

Luke titled his head and quirked a brow. "You've been stalking me while I shower?" he asked. He didn't seem upset by the idea, more amused and...intrigued?

-I'm pleading the fifth on that one, pup...- Dean winked one yellow eye. *-but even if I haven't, you sing* very *loudly and I have* very *good ears. I can hear you clear across town-*

"Oh fuck off."

-Hey, at least you're a good singer. If you sounded like a parakeet in a blender, I might have had to intervene-

Luke smirked and then shook himself, finally getting back around to his original point.

"As I was saying, we'll go a little further into the woods and find somewhere to camp for the night. I think another day's walk and we'll be close enough to start doing recon."

They all agreed and trudged onward. The walk through the woods was far more enjoyable than the one through the desert. The over-arching branches and crimson leaves provided a nice canopy to shelter them from the glaring sun and a reprieve from the stifling heat. Eventually they came upon a wide stream, a small clearing near its bank, and decided it was as good a spot as any to camp for the night.

"I've been smelling some kind of game ever since we entered the woods. I'm going to go hunt. I'm sure we could all use a break from gel packs and granola bars for dinner."

"I will give you every winning lottery number for the next fifty years if you bring me *anything* else to eat," Emmie said, her mouth watering at the idea of some actual food. Luke chuckled and Dean stalked towards him.

-I'll come with you-

Luke grinned. "Try to keep up, kitten."

-You'll pay for that, pup-

"Emmie, I have zero doubts that you can defend yourself, but stay alert. I don't smell anyone else, but you never know."

"Of course," she said, warmth filling her chest. The fact that Luke didn't think she was some kind of damsel in distress that needed constant rescuing or protecting made her love him even more. It was flattering that he understood how powerful she was, and that he didn't seem threatened by it. On the contrary. He seemed enthralled by it, proud even. It was the way Dean had always looked at her as well. Not as someone to be hidden away behind glass, but as someone who would break the glass and slit your throat with the shards herself if you didn't watch your step. On the flip side, she knew that both of them would still always put themselves between her and any perceived threat, and that was equally loveable.

Luke transformed and the boys sped off into the woods, two dark blurs among the darker trees. Emmie went about constructing a nice little lean-to out of some of the monstrous trees nearby. Alright, so it was a very upscale lean to. More like a three-walled cabin, the open front draped with a curtain made from the crimson leaves and an opening in the roof to allow smoke to escape.

"Not too shabby," she said to herself, dusting her hands off on each other, as if she'd actually lifted a finger to physically do any of the work. Her phasing might not be working right here and her visions might be a little haywire, but at least some of her powers still seemed to be functioning just fine.

She stowed their bags, set out their blankets, and started a fire.

She eyed the stream and smiled.

"And now, I'd say it's time for a bath."

CHAPTER
EIGHT

Running with Lucas in his wolf form was exhilarating. A normal cat would never have been able to keep up with Luke's incredible speed, but being a demigod in cat's clothing had its perks. The two of them shot through the woods like two streaks of black lightning. Dean felt completely free and it made his breath catch. *Gods, when was the last time I felt like this? Too long.*

-Alright, alright. Stop trying to show off. We have dinner to catch, pup-

Luke chuckled. *-I wasn't even at three-quarters speed-*

Dean could hear the cocky tone of Luke's voice inside his head and he rolled his eyes, but grinned inwardly. Cocky could be very, *very* sexy when it was done properly. And Luke did it like a pro.

They both slowed, using their enhanced senses to reach out and locate their prey.

-Smell that? About a mile due west-

Dean nodded and they began running that direction, both of them silent in their pursuit. When they neared, Dean pulled ahead and took to the trees, gliding through the branches like a panther. When he spotted them, he settled on a thick branch and spied down.

ward: a group of something that looked a bit like oversized pheas-
ants was poking around in the dirt.

-*Eight of them*- Dean told Luke. -*Watch out for the claws*- he added,
spying the talons on one of the creatures. At least six inches long and
razor sharp, judging by the way the moonlight glinted off of the dark
edge.

-*On it*-

Dean watched in fascination and awe as Luke leapt into the
small clearing, teeth and claws bared, moving like liquid midnight
and with a grace that a creature so large shouldn't possess. He was
beautiful. Deadly and terrifying, of course, but absolutely beautiful.
He made short work of the animals and soon they were headed back
with five out of the eight ready to be plucked and cooked. Dean's
mouth watered at the idea of fresh meat.

But as they entered their campsite, Dean and Lucas both froze,
all thoughts of a warm meal evaporating from Dean's head. Emmie
was bathing in the stream, her bare back to them, and she looked like
a painting of some kind of water deity of old. The moonlight shone
done, bathing her in silvery-blue light that made her tattoos
shimmer and glow as if they were liquid mercury. Her long, silver
hair was pulled over one shoulder and water trickled down her back.
Dean longed to trace the path of the droplets down her spine with
his fingers and his tongue with a force that staggered him.

"Fuck," Luke whisper-groaned, wiping a hand over his mouth
and through the scruff on his chin.

-*I second that*- Dean said, swallowing thickly.

Don't turn around. He silently begged. *Don't turn...I don't think
I can—*

She turned ever so slightly, the outline of one breast visible
now.

-*GODS*- Dean groaned. It had been too fucking long. He'd had...
needs over the centuries, of course, but he'd managed to deal with
them, to put mind over matter. But lately, that had been getting
harder and harder. Now, seeing Emmie's pert breast, her nipple

jutting and just begging for his lips...Well, it was nearly un-fucking-bearable.

When Luke made a low growling sound in his chest, Emmie glanced over her shoulder. Even in the low light, Dean knew damn well that Luke could see the amused, sensual flirtation in her gaze as well as he could.

"Hello, boys," she said in a low voice. "Why don't you make dinner while I finish up here?"

Luke cleared his throat and, after a moment and what appeared to be a great effort, shifted his gaze away from Emmie. He made his way around to the front of the impressive shelter that she'd made in their absence. It was basically a small cabin with an open front covered in a curtain of leaves, and a fire was already burning high within it, ready to cook their dinner. Dean watched Emmie turn her back to him once more and splash water over her body before he shook himself and joined Luke.

Luke began expertly plucking the feathers from the strange birds and Dean watched him work, lost in his own thoughts for a bit.

"It must be hard for you," Luke said after a few minutes. "To deal with not being able to...well, you know." He seemed to be trying a little too hard to seem nonchalant while he worked on the last bird.

-*To fuck?*- Dean asked, amused.

Luke choked in surprise, coughing a few times. Dean laughed inside Luke's mind, and Luke's lips curled upward. He gathered up the now naked birds, and made his way inside the cabin to begin roasting them on a small spit over the flames. Dean studied him. Luke was normally all confidence and sexy swagger among mortals and supernatural beings, but Dean had found that around the gods and himself and Emmie, Luke had a new vulnerability about him, an almost shyness that was actually really endearing.

-*Sometimes it's harder than others*- Dean couldn't stop himself from glancing towards the stream again, though with the way the cabin was situated, he couldn't see Emmie.

"I can't imagine. I can't imagine anything you've been through."

Luke met his gaze, the green standing out brightly in his eyes as it always did after he changed, and said with an intense surety, "We *will* fix this, Dean. We'll get the curse lifted and you can have your life back. And..." He looked away, staring into the fire. "And if she chooses you, I'll be ok with that. I'll...somehow make myself be ok with that," he amended. "Because you deserve her. You deserve...well you deserve that and more after everything. I want that for you, Dean. I want..."

He looked up from the fire again and their gazes collided. The air seemed to vanish from the space around them, everything suddenly thick and heavy and Dean's heart started thudding loudly in his chest. Was Dean imagining the thick tension? Was he imagining how Luke's eyes darkened, how the pulse point at his throat jumped?

"I want..." Luke swallowed hard and shifted his gaze away again, clearing his throat. "I just want you both to be happy," he finished.

Dean blinked several times, not quite sure what to say. The moment that had just passed between them had been...something. Hadn't it? Or was it wishful thinking? Was that really all Luke had wanted to say, that he wanted Dean to be happy?

Before he could say anything, Emmie ducked into the structure, inhaling deeply. She was dressed again, thankfully (unfortunately?), her damp hair pulled up into a loose knot on the top of her head, droplets of water dripping down onto her shoulders over the thin straps of her tank top.

"It smells amazing," she said with a dreamy look in her purple eyes as she settled on the other side of the fire.

Luke met Dean's gaze and then smiled at Emmie, the moment between them fading and drifting away with the smoke from the fire.

"Well, hope you're hungry."

CHAPTER
NINE

After another day of hiking, they finally found themselves near the mountain.

"We need to find somewhere to make a good camp. This close to the compound, we need to be sure it's secure and able to be defended easily, just in case. They might send patrols out beyond the pass. We'll need to scout for a couple of days at least before heading in," Luke said, eyeing the staggered peaks of the soaring mountain above the tree line a couple of miles away.

Emmie started to suggest splitting up, but froze as a vision rose up in her mind. This wasn't a new vision, it was the memory of one from long ago: her brother standing in front of a black, jagged rock face, ropes of thick vines covered in razor-sharp thorns hanging over the surface like a curtain, gnarled black trees with blood-red leaves in the background, and Allister's runes flaring to life with silver-blue light as he waved his hands over the vines...

She'd nearly forgotten about the vision. It had been centuries ago, she thought, maybe longer. It was hard to keep track. Sometimes a decade felt like a millennium, and others it felt like an hour.

Her lips curled upward as she remembered the vision and the conversation they'd had about it years later:

"Where on earth were you?" Emmie asked after explaining the vision to her brother, "and what were you doing?"

"You'll need a safe place one day, and so I made you one," he said with a cryptic smile. "That's all I'm telling you. Unlike you, I don't like to meddle."

"Oh please, you like to meddle just as much as I do, you just aren't as good at it." He smiled at her, the full, unabashed smile that made his whole face shine like the sun. The smile he'd worn almost nonstop when he and Hermes had been together...

She blinked as the memory faded, and the love for her brother surged within her like a tidal wave, crashing against the inside of her chest and filling her entire body with warmth. The list of beings that Emmie would kill or die for without a moment's thought seemed to be growing exponentially as of late, but Allister would always be at the top of it.

"I know where we have to go." She took off, leading the boys through the thick trees, looking for the signs only she could see. They crossed the same stream from before, but it was wider here, more like a small river. The water was shockingly colder than it had been farther from the mountain and Emmie grumbled about cold, wet feet as they continued on their path.

"Emmie, are you sure—"

"Here!" she called, sprinting ahead of them and grinning at their muttered curses of exasperation both in her ears and her mind. She came upon the rock face from her vision. It was a section of Black Mountain that curled out to the west like a long tentacle, curving along the outside border of the forest. Jagged stones covered the surface, shades of black and gray, with streaks of glittering crystal at intervals, shimmering brighter now than they had in her vision. Vines crept up the rocks here and there, a few trees even becoming emboldened enough to grow directly out of the side of the mountain itself.

And there, just in front of Emmie, was the wall of thorns where Allister had stood decades before. The vines were thicker here than on other parts of the mountain side, nearly as big around as her arm, and the thorns looked downright menacing. Thick, scarlet liquid slowly dripped down the vines and thorns, looking all too much like someone had tried and failed to make their way through.

"Whoa," Luke breathed from just behind her on her right. She felt Dean come to stand just on her left.

-Is that...blood?-

Emmie tilted her head, moving closer to the vines and inhaling deeply.

"It's bloodberry sap," she laughed. "I had no idea bloodberries grew anywhere but Mount Olympus, but that is definitely what these are." They were some of her favorites and could make the absolute best wine...

She reached out and plucked a berry, a few shades lighter than the liquid running down the thorns, from one of the vines and popped it in her mouth. She moaned in delight. She grabbed a few more and held them out to Luke. He took them, looking a little skeptical, but popped one in his mouth. His eyes flew wide.

"Holy shit, that's good," he said, throwing another one in his mouth while offering another to Dean who took a small bite.

-They do taste great, I'll give you that, love. But...how does this help us with a place to camp?-

Emmie closed her eyes and reached out with her power, sensing the magics at work here, the source of them, the nature of them, the purpose...the steep price to be paid for trying to breach them uninvited. Thankfully, Allister had seen that Emmie would need plus-ones to this party, and she knew that Dean, Lucas, and even Sabina would be allowed entry to this place.

Emmie could feel Allister all around her, his latent power calling out to her own. She missed her brother so much, a constant dull ache in her chest. She still saw him often, and leaving the Fates had been the best decision for both of them, but sometimes she longed for those times, when she was with him every day, when she didn't feel like a piece of herself was always missing.

He'd moved to the Mortal Plane centuries ago, saying that being in any of the godly planes was just too difficult after the fall out between him and Hermes. Of course, that had all been one giant misunderstanding, but sometimes the damage done was too much to come back from, even when the damage was accidental. She'd seen possible reconciliation in the future, but they were shifting too much to be sure. Too many decisions left to be made to be certain of what was to come, but she hoped that what she'd seen would come to pass. She wanted Allister happy, and if he could stop being so damn stubborn, he could be again, she was...ninety-two percent sure of it.

She sighed and turned the lock within her mind, opening the mystical wards. Her eyes snapped open and with a flick of her fingers, the vines parted down the middle like a curtain. Just beyond the opening was a short tunnel of stone, but beyond that, Emmie could see light. Bright light. Much brighter than the light here on the other side within the trees.

With a grin, she darted through, the boys hot on her heels and grumbling about running into places that they hadn't cleared yet. She rolled her eyes and laughed, but it quickly cut off on a soft gasp as she emerged from the tunnel.

Before her stood a large, circular space, surrounded on all sides by soaring stone walls, but unlike the black and gray stone outside, here it was a mix of pale blue, purple, and silver. A small waterfall cascaded from inside one of the walls, forming small lake on the far side of the clearing. Magic obviously kept the water at a steady level despite the ever-flowing water coming in. The grass all around them was green and lush, and flowers of all shapes, sizes, and colors dotted the landscape. A path of crushed white shells led from the tunnel to a large house.

Or a small manor, she supposed. She tilted her head, brow furrowing. It very much looked like—

"Is that...Mr. Darcy's house?" Lucas asked. Emmie and Dean both turned quizzical looks on him, and his cheeks flushed. He was so cute when he blushed. "Skylar made me watch it," he grumbled defensively. "Shut up, both of you." He strode forward, but Emmie heard him mutter under his breath, "As if *anyone* is immune to that Darcy hand-flex..."

Emmie pulled her lips in to hide her smile and Dean chuckled within her mind as they followed Luke towards the house that was, in fact, a small replica of Pemberley, the one from the Kiera Knightly version, to be precise. *Allister does have a flare for the dramatic*, she thought with a grin.

They entered the house and lights flared to life all around them. Though the outside screamed early nineteenth century England, the inside was modern and cozy, laid out like an open-floor plan farm house, with exposed beams and rustic, yet chic, décor. Mystical fire roared to life within the fireplace in the large living room and Emmie rushed forward, yanking off her sodden boots and sighing in relief at the painful-pleasure feeling in her toes of the cold being chased away by the flames.

-*I'm going to explore*- Dean said, darting off silent as death.

"Are you alright?" Luke asked, voice soft.

Emmie sighed. "I am. Tired. But being here, I can feel my brother and it helps."

Luke nodded and hefted one of the oversized chairs closer to the fire, urging her to sit. She thought about protesting, but gave in instead. As soon as her ass hit the cushion, exhaustion settled over her like she'd just put on a heavy coat. Her lids felt like they weighed twenty pounds and, no sooner had Luke covered her with a soft, fleece blanket and kissed her softly on the forehead, was she dragged under into the darkness.

～

"ARE YOU SURE ABOUT THIS?" Luke asked in a low voice. They crouched behind an old mining cart that had been discarded decades ago after the cult took over the compound. After two and a half days of recon, the boys had deemed it time to move in.

-It's the best plan and you know it, pup-

"You only don't like it because you have to play the prisoner," Emmie pointed out with a grin. She'd caught flashes of the plan and it appeared to be a solid one, but she couldn't be completely sure with the realm only giving her choppy pieces. It was like an old VHS tape where wobbly or static-filled bits popped up every now and then, obscuring the video.

In watching the compound, they'd seen the goblins leading prisoners—or more accurately, sacrifices—from one of the many small outbuildings lining the edges of the compound towards the enormous, temple-like structure that had been erected in the center of the hollowed-out mountain. It hadn't been easy to watch and not intervene, but Emmie tried to console herself with knowing that they would save as many as they could soon enough.

She personally planned to make every last goblin in this gods forsaken place beg for mercy before she denied it—and ripped their tongues out for daring to even ask. Hurting innocents was not something she tolerated, and these cultists had done it in droves. They needed to be punished accordingly, and she was all too happy to be judge, jury, and executioner.

So, they planned to waltz right in with Emmie transformed into one of the cultist guards, and Lucas posing as a sacrifice that had been captured. The goblins didn't appear to be all that bright and the guard that she was transforming into seemed to be of a higher rank than many of the others from what they could tell, so they were fairly certain that they could walk in without raising much suspicion.

"Fine," Luke grated, rolling his eyes. "Let's get this done."

Emmie grinned and took a deep breath. She threw a faint glamour over him to make it look as if he were much shorter with far less muscle mass. She added a bruised cheek and bloody lip for good measure, mussed his hair, and tore his shirt a bit at the collar. She couldn't stop herself from leaning up and placing a soft kiss at the base of his throat and grinned when he shivered. She knew she shouldn't tease him, knew how tightly strung he still was from their little escapade in the cave without any release of his own, but, well, she had very little control over herself when Luke was nearby. *Sue me.*

She tied his wrists behind his back with a thick leather cord, loose enough that he could easily get himself free, but giving the appearance that he was bound and fully under control.

-Bondage, I like it- Dean teased playfully, that sensual purr in his voice that had nothing to do with being a cat.

"Never knew you were into that," Luke responded, but his voice was a bit rougher than usual.

-Oh, I could teach you things beyond your wildest imaginings, pup-

Luke's eyes widened a fraction and he swallowed hard before seeming to shake himself. He turned away to scan the area in front of the temple. Dean winked at Emmie and she chuckled silently before pushing her shoulders back and putting her game face on.

"Alright, here we go," Emmie breathed just before letting the transformation settle over her. It felt a bit like icy water flowing over her entire body, starting in the center of her scalp and slowly trickling downward, and what was left in its wake was whatever form she'd selected. The initial shock of the change wasn't comfortable, exactly, but she was so used to it now that it barely even registered, and after those first few heartbeats, she felt only a faint pulsing sensation for as long as she held the form. Transforming was as easy as breathing and took hardly any concentration for the first few hours. After that, it took a bit more power, but if necessary, she could hold another form for a few days. That was under normal circumstances. Here, she would be lucky to be able to hold it for a couple of hours without draining herself completely. This realm was really screwing with her and she didn't appreciate it at all. She cut her eyes skyward and scowled, wondering if Zarafina was behind this some-how. It seemed like something she would do if she could.

"Whoa, that's freaky," Luke said, eyeing her goblin-form up and down.

"Aw, come on, you don't find this sexy?" she asked, voice coming out in a low, rough growl that sounded like a bunch nuts and bolts thrown in a blender on high speed. Emmie grimaced. "Well, *that's* attractive."

-Ok you two, focus. Be safe. I'll be right behind you.-

With that, Emmie and Luke stepped from behind the cart and Dean darted into the shadows of a nearby pillar. There weren't many goblins milling about outside, but two guards stood at the large entrance of the temple. When they neared, Emmie shoved Luke forcefully, and he stumbled dramatically, appearing to be exhausted and beaten into submission.

"Another one?" one of the guards asked.

Emmie nodded. The shorter guard narrowed his eyes.

"Stryand didn't say anything about another sacrifice today."

"I don't give two flying shites what Stryand said. This piece of trash tried to escape," she growled, kicking out at the back of Luke's leg, making him fall to one knee on the stone slab before the door. "Now, he gets to lose his worthless life in honor of Valen." At the name, all three of them bowed their heads and thumped a closed fist over their chest three times, chanting *blessed be her name*. Emmie wanted to puke.

She sent the shorter guard a withering look, and he averted his eyes, stepping aside at the same time as the other one to allow her and Luke entrance into the temple without another word. They didn't know the layout of the inside, but they did know they needed to get to the west side of the compound, near the fountain Emmie had heard in her vision. They'd found it easily once they reached the compound, and now Emmie let Lucas lead her the right way—she was terrible with directions.

They passed several more guards clad in what was apparently

the goblin soldier uniform: leather pants, tunic-type sleeveless shirts with thick leather straps crossing their chests, with swords thrust through them. Each one inclined their heads to her, not raising a brow at her or her prisoner.

They also saw goblins in hooded robes the color of sand exiting an enormous, darkened room. When they passed the doorway, Emmie bit the inside of her cheek to keep herself from reacting: inside, on an alter on a raised dais, was a body, blood pouring down its lifeless chest and dripping onto—

"What the fuck," Luke swore in a low voice, his body tensing and his claws shooting free from the tips of his fingers. Emmie couldn't see his face, but she knew his fangs would have lengthened as well, his eyes starting to turn wholly gold as the change threatened to overtake him.

The blood dripped onto a *pile* of bodies, scattered around the alter like trash. Ten, fifteen maybe. Emmie swallowed hard against the bile and rage rising in her throat, but forced herself to keep moving. They needed to find Sabina. They needed to lift Dean's curse.

Then, they'd kill all these fuckers.

CHAPTER
TEN

"I can hear the fountain. We've gotta be close..."

-Took you long enough-

Sitting in front of thick wooden door, flicking his tail and somehow gloating even as a fucking cat, was Dean.

"Aw, look at the pretty kitty," Lucas crooned.

-I'll scratch your eyes out, pup-

Despite the situation, despite what he and Emmie had just seen and whatever the hell was about to come, Luke laughed. It seemed Dean could always make him laugh, even when he didn't want to, even when he was pissed, even when no one else on the planet could, not even Skylar.

"Alright, let's check it out." Emmie moved forward and placed her hand on the iron handle, but paused. She turned to Dean. "Are you ready?"

The weight of her words seemed to settle over them, slowly at first, and then all at once, like the first few flakes of snow falling off a roof before the entire sheet slides down in a rush. This was it. Dean was about to be himself once more. His torment was about to end. And Luke felt like he might fucking cry from the intense joy he felt for his friend. He barely stopped himself from rubbing the heel of his hand against his chest, trying to stop the strange ache there.

Dean let out a long, slow breath and then nodded.

-I'm ready, love-

They silently slipped through the doorway and down a long set of worn stone stairs that eventually let out onto a wide, dim hallway. The air was thick and musty, and though torches were set into iron rings every few feet, most of them weren't burning. The floor was packed earth and Emmie let out a small yelp as rats scurried past them.

"Want a snack, Dean?" Luke said in a low voice. He tried to make his tone light, but he was shot through with tension.

-If all goes to plan, you won't be able to make jokes like that much longer, pup-

They spread out, each checking out the numerous cells lining the corridor, but they were all empty and looked like they had been for quite a while. Maybe they were wrong, maybe the vision was of somewhere else.

"Are we sure—"

"Here," Emmie called from the very end of the hallway.

A sharp voice rang out from within the cell.

"What do you want, you disgusting little..." The voice trailed off as Emmie shivered, the goblin form fading away and her true self standing tall and beautiful and practically glowing amid the dingy surroundings. "What the *fuck*?"

Dean and Luke exchanged a quick, meaningful glance and then sprinted forward, coming to stand on either side of Emmie. A woman stood inside the cell. A ragged, gray dress hung off of her slim body, and her hair stood out in tangled curls around her face. Luke thought it was probably an alluring shade of red when it wasn't coated in what looked like decades of grime. Her cheek bones were sharp and angular, as if she were nearly starved, with dark circles beneath her eyes, like bruises.

Her eyes, though dim with exhaustion and what Luke would

imagine was defeat, were a startling turquoise color that he'd never seen before. Her skin was deathly pale and covered with smears of dirt, but Luke could see the beauty beneath the ragged appearance. When she wasn't being held captive in a dungeon, she would surely be breathtaking.

A silver shackle was clamped over one ankle, a thick chain running from it to a rod set into the back wall of the cell. She could walk back and forth across the length of the cell, but couldn't get any closer to the door.

Before Emmie or Luke could say anything more, Dean bared his fangs and hissed.

-YOU FUCKING BITCH!- he roared inside all of their minds.

With that, he flew through the bars, moving so fast he was merely a blur of black, and launched himself at Sabina's neck—claws poised to rip out her throat.

RAGE EXPLODED within Dean's chest upon seeing Sabina. Five hundred years' worth of it. He launched himself at her without thought, wanting nothing more than to pluck her eyes from their sockets, to claw out her tongue, to make her suffer as he had suffered and then some.

She screamed and tried to move away, but she was chained to the wall, only able to maneuver so much. It was enough that his claws raked across her chest rather than her face, though. Not what he'd wanted, but seeing her blood spilling down the front of her rags was satisfying enough to momentarily quell his fury. She managed to throw him off and he skitted along the dirty floor, digging in his claws to slow his movements and turn to glower at her.

"What the fuck!?" she shrieked as Lucas ripped open the cell door as if it were nothing and he and Emmie barreled inside. Dean tensed his muscles to leap again, but Emmie threw herself between

them, and Lucas positioned himself slightly in front of Dean, in a...
protective stance? Was he afraid the witch was going to retaliate?

"Dean—knock it off. She can't lift the curse if you slice her jugu-
lar. Sabina—shut up unless you want an entire cult's worth of
goblins heading down here to interrupt our rescue mission."

Sabina's eyes blazed as she glared at Dean, but then her mouth
popped open as Emmie's words really registered. She snapped her
head in Emmie's direction, the murderous cat momentarily
forgotten apparently.

"Rescue mission?"

Then she really seemed to see Emmie for the first time, blinking
as she took in Emmie's runed skin, the power emanating from her.
Sabina had the good sense to relax her defensive posture and take a
small step backwards.

"So long as you agree to a few stipulations, yes, we'll bust you
out of these...lovely accommodations," Emmie said, curling her lip a
little as she surveyed the cell, but then she grinned wickedly, eyes
lighting up. "Then we're going to murder every last one of these
bastards and burn this vile facsimile of a place of worship to the
ground. Maybe piss on the ashes if the mood strikes. You'll be
welcome to join in—*if* you cooperate."

Sabina swallowed hard, though her eyes flared in excitement at
the mention of destroying the Order.

"What do you want from me?" she asked, eyeing the three of
them warily. Her gaze lingered on Dean for a moment, confusion
flashing in her eyes. He glared at her, hissing and baring his fangs
again. He stalked back and forth but Luke moved with him, always
keeping himself between Dean and Sabina.

-I don't need protecting, pup- Dean grumbled.

"It's not you I'm protecting, idiot," he shot back in a low voice.
"We need her, remember?"

Sabina heard the one-sided conversation and looked more
confused than ever.

"We need you to lift the curse you placed on our companion

here." Emmie glanced towards Dean and Lucas. "The furry one," she clarified and then frowned. "Although, technically, the tall one becomes furry at times too...but I mean the cat."

"What in the name of Hekate are you talking about? What curse?"

-The one you put on me almost five hundred years ago, you bitch. All because you thought *I fucked someone else in your coven and wouldn't even let me explain-*

Luke's head snapped up, eyes narrowing at Sabina as Dean's words sounded in all of their minds.

"*That's* why you cursed him? Because you thought he slept with one of your friends? *Seriously!?*" His claws shot long again, agitation making his muscles tense and bulge, incredulity and anger making his voice rough and harsh. Something about his reaction made Dean's chest heat and twist.

-Something I didn't even fucking do, might I add!-

Sabina's brow furrowed.

"I don't..." She gasped quietly as her eyes flew wide in shock as realization struck, her jaw going slack. "Conan?" she whispered.

-I go by Dean now, but yes- he grated.

"Oh my gods. I...I..." She cast her eyes downward and a faint blush colored her pale cheeks. "I'm sorry." Dean's head reared back, surprised by the response. She rolled her eyes. "I acted rashly—I was young! Only three hundred or so!" When three sets of eyes narrowed at her, she quickly added, "But I know that's no excuse. I was a jealous person and you were...Well, I know that it was mere fun for you, but I thought I had a claim of sorts. Again, I was young and foolish. I'd just gained my queendom, I thought I was owed, well, anything and everything I wanted. I was..."

"Pigheaded and entitled?" Emmie said.

"A heinous bitch?" Luke suggested.

She pressed her lips into a thin line, clearly agitated.

"Perhaps both of those things, yes," she admitted. "I *did* get the truth out of Dannika later and I planned to find you and remove the curse...but then I was taken by these fucking insane sycophants." She threw her arm wide, gesturing to the temple full of goblins above them. "I've been stuck here ever since."

"Remove the curse. *Now*," Luke demanded. His entire body seemed to vibrate with tension and rage, and Dean could tell that he was barely stopping himself from turning.

Sabina paled, shrinking away from Luke's massive form.

"I..." She swallowed hard, fear flashing in her turquoise eyes. "I can't."

"I swear to all the gods..." Luke growled, taking half a step forward.

"I swear on Hekate's name that I'm not lying! I would lift it if I could, I promise you, but I can't. I *literally* can't." Luke and Dean both rolled their eyes, but Emmie's narrowed in suspicion.

"Why?" she asked.

Sabina bit her lip, eyes darting as if she were torn between answering them and burrowing through the floor just to get away.

"I can't tell you," she finally whispered. "It's the greatest secret of my people. I cannot divulge—"

"The knowledge never leaves this room," Emmie said quickly, seeming to understand. "We will all make a blood vow right here, right now if that's what it takes. Whatever secret you're holding will never be known by anyone but your kind and the three of us standing here."

Dean's heart was racing. He felt so close, as if he were trudging up a mountain side, so close to the top that he could spy the highest peak just out of reach. Sabina eyed each of them intently and then sighed, shoulders slumping as if the weight of the world sat upon it.

"An Enchantress has innate power and magic, but when she comes of age, it manifests too strongly to be held within her body. It must be contained in an object enchanted, blessed, and bound by the entire strength of the coven. Without that object, an Enchantress has only limited power."

"What?" Luke asked, brows shooting skyward. "But...Someone would have noticed, someone would have figured that out..."

Sabina shook her head. "It can be something as small as a ring or necklace, a hair clip, a bracelet. No one would think twice about seeing someone wear jewelry, especially our kind. It's one reason we all wear as much of it as possible usually, to hide our power in plain sight. It isn't *all* about vanity, though, that is a part of it."

It was true that enchanters were known for their affinity for adornments, the more sparkly, the better. Men and women alike didn't leave the house without at least ten pieces on, often times more. *What clever little witches*, Dean thought.

"*Holy shit,*" Luke breathed as he came to the same realization. That kind of knowledge could be disastrous if it fell into the wrong hands.

"So," Sabina continued, sighing heavily, "I cannot lift the curse because I don't have enough innate power left in my veins without my amulet and those fuckers took it from me. They meant to destroy it so I told them it was Valen's herself—a family heirloom, which, coincidentally is actually true—and that she could never return if they destroyed it. They took it to their sacred temple—not this monstrosity where they do their dirty work—high up in the peaks of the mountain. Rumor is that it's guarded by a beast terrifying enough to scare even gods and is full of traps and pitfalls."

And just like that, Dean felt as if he were tumbling down the mountain side, the peak moving farther and farther out of reach. *I was so close, so fucking close—*

"What if you draw from another's power?" Emmie asked, her tattoos flaring brighter as if to punctuate her sentence, and Dean froze in his metaphorical fall, clinging to Emmie's words in a desperate attempt to stop his descent into the darkness that was threatening to close in on him.

Sabina's eyes flew wide. "Yes, I think...yes, that could work."

"Ok, so new plan: we lift the curse, the three of us," she indicated to herself, Dean, and Luke, "go find your amulet then come back to rescue you—again. After that, we commence with the slaughtering and the burning and the pissing on the ashes. *Then* we all go home and maybe grab some wings and a few beers on the way. Oh! Wait, you need to lift another pesky little curse from a dear friend once we get there too. Then a wedding, and *then* wings and beers."

Sabina blinked, trying to absorb everything Emmie was saying and probably only understanding about half of it. Dean knew that buffalo wings and beers were definitely not a thing when Sabina was captured. She shook off everything she didn't get and instead focused on what seemed to be the most important, her eyes looking panicked.

"Why do you have to come back for me? I'll come with you, I can help—"

-You just said the amulet is guarded by beasties on some treacherous mountain peak and admitted that you have basically no power. You can't help- Dean didn't mean to sound so cold and bitter, but it was difficult. This was the woman who had fucked his entire life for half a millennium because of a bout of unwarranted jealousy. Part of him was even delighted at the fact that she'd been suffering all this time as well, powerless as he (mostly) was. *Turnabout's a bitch, bitch.*

"*Bitch, bitch.* Got that?" Luke muttered quietly, his lips quirking up a tiny bit on one side. *Fuck, I'd said that in his head? I hadn't even realized...*

-Shut it, pup-

"And, more importantly," Emmie said, clearly trying to keep the peace, though Dean could tell that she wasn't thrilled with Sabina either, "it will take us time to retrieve it. If they come down here and find you gone, it will raise alarms and make all our lives more difficult." Emmie's eyes went unfocused for a moment and she shuddered. "Yep, it's no good. You have to stay put."

Sabina looked like she wanted to protest, but then her shoulders slumped.

"You're right," she sighed.

"I usually am," Emmie agreed.

"We need to do this now and get out of here before we're caught," Luke said walking to the door of the cell and glancing down the long hallway, looking tense and alert, every bit the assassin and mercenary he'd been trained to be.

Sabina nodded. "Yes, alright." She looked to Emmie and the ghost of a smile passed over her face. "I'm sorry, we never got around to introductions."

"Emmie," she said and then jerked her head towards Luke, "and Lucas"

"Well, if you can truly restore my amulet and get me out of this place, then it will be very nice to have met you, indeed." Luke stepped back into the cell and crossed his arms over his massive chest, waiting expectantly.

"That all hinges on if you can lift the curse. If not, have fun staying here for the rest of eternity," he said, voice cold.

Sabina pressed her lips into a hard line again.

"I know you won't believe me, but I truly *am* sorry. I never would have let you suffer all this time if I could have helped it. And I can do it, I can lift the curse—with a little help. Let's get started." She turned to Emmie. "Your hand, if you please."

Emmie stepped forward and extended her hand. When Sabina grasped it, Emmie's runes flared brightly and Sabina gasped, color immediately returning to her pale skin.

"Dear *goddess*, what are you?" she asked, her voice filled with wonder and sounding honestly a bit lust-drunk. Dean supposed it was like abstaining from coffee for years and years only to down thirty espresso shots in a row...times about a thousand.

"The world may never know," Emmie said cryptically, grinning.

Sabina shuddered and then gestured to Dean.

"Conan—er, Dean," she corrected quickly at Luke's glare and low growl rumbling in his chest, "come closer."

Dean stalked forward with as much dignity as he could muster and sat in front of the bitch.

"This will most likely be...ah, less than pleasant since it's been a part of you for so long."

-Just do it-

"Alright then."

She nodded and took a few deep breaths, preparing herself Dean guessed. She raised her palms towards him, closing her eyes. Emmie's runes shone brightly in the dark cell, acting like a battery for Sabina's power, and Dean could never thank her enough for this. For everything.

He felt the magic begin to flow over him, a soft tingling sensation, cold at first but gradually warming.

A moment later, the pain began.

CHAPTER
ELEVEN

Luke tensed as every muscle in Dean's body went rigid, his back bowing under the strain, claws digging into the packed earth floor. Sabina said it would be painful, and by the looks of it, that had been an understatement. Emmie looked distraught, but held fast to Sabina's hand, sharing her god-like power with the Enchantress. An unnatural wind began to swirl through the cell, kicking up sand and dust, and soon a small cyclone of pale gray, translucent smoke enveloped Dean.

Luke stepped forward, his need to protect Dean rearing up, stronger than ever before. He didn't quite understand it, but he couldn't deny the instincts that were screaming at him, practically clawing at his chest, demanding that he do something to stop Dean's pain.

He forced himself to stop and held himself rigidly as he watched. This *had* to happen. This was a *good* thing. What was it Emmie always said? Sometimes you had to be cruel to be kind. That may be the truth, but Luke didn't fucking like it.

He ground his teeth so hard his jaw hurt, and when a scream tore through his mind, his claws shot out, slicing into his palms where his fists were clenched at his sides. Hot blood flowed between his fingers and dripped to the ground, but still, he remained where he was, muscles locked and trembling. For the thousandth time in his life, Luke silently thanked Dalton for the countless hours of training he'd put Lucas through, teaching him to master his body and mind, making sure he could handle anything that may come his way.

"Almost," Sabina panted. She was sweating, her frail body shaking and looking like it was nearly ready to give out. As if in answer to Sabina's weakness, Emmie's runes flared brighter, silver light hoovering around her as she forced strength into the Enchantress. "Almost...almost..."

The smoke swirled faster and faster, and just when another scream ricocheted through Luke's mind and he was determined to put an end to this torture, everything just...stopped. The dust and dirt froze, suspended weightless in the air for an endless moment, and then everything collapsed with a resounding whoosh, sending a wave of energy crashing through the cell. Luke turned his head, leaning forward to avoid being shoved backwards from the force of it.

When he turned back, he lost his breath.

There, on hands and knees, fingers digging into the earth and spasms racking his body, was...Dean. The *real* Dean. No more pointed ears, no more swishy tail, no more black fur. He was a man. Or a demigod, more accurately, but he looked like a man. A tattoo ran down the length of his spine, something in an ancient language that Luke had no hope of understanding, but the characters somehow spoke to him of a warrior's spirit, of strength and cunning and wisdom.

Sabina collapsed then, going down hard on her knees, panting and swaying. Emmie's eyes were wide, her hand shaking slightly as she raised it to her mouth.

"Dean?" she whispered.

Slowly, Dean raised his head and sat back on his knees. He was shirtless, in worn leather pants that hung low on his trim body. He had broad shoulders, nearly as broad as Luke's own, but they tapered down to a narrower waist, the muscles at the base of his spine forming a small "V." His hair was blonde and shaggy, brushing the tops of his shoulders.

"Meow?" Dean said weakly, his voice rough. With that, a strangled sob broke free from Emmie's throat. She rushed forward and dropped to her knees, throwing her arms around Dean and nearly knocking him over. Dean hugged her back so fiercely, burying his face in her neck, that Luke suddenly felt like he was trespassing on something intimate. He looked away, his throat feeling thick, an empty feeling settling in his stomach.

He was about to lose her.

He was about to lose them *both*.

For weeks now, they'd been an almost inseparable trio, and now he could hardly imagine them being apart...didn't *want* to imagine it. He didn't want to think about going back to his apartment and one or both of them not being there. He didn't want to think about binge watching TV without them, didn't want to imagine trying to talk weapons and battle tactics with anyone but Dean, didn't want to learn about the entire new world of the gods from anyone but Emmie.

But now...was he about to be a weird third wheel? He was already that with Skylar and Hades sometimes, and he had a feeling that he was heading that direction with Zahara and Zeus too. Was this his fate? To constantly be on the outside of love? To see it but never actually touch it?

Just when Luke was seriously considering ducking out into the corridor to give them a minute and contemplate his entire existence in a very melodramatic fashion like a fucking tool, Dean pulled away from Emmie. He rose to his feet and turned to Lucas. Their gazes locked and something seemed to click into place, something... profound. Something Lucas couldn't fully comprehend in the moment. The muted mating instincts he'd been having about Emmie suddenly screamed to life, sharp in their clarity and perfection...but there were also additional instincts. Instincts about *Dean*. Instincts that couldn't be right...could they?

Luke tried to think if he'd ever read any account of a wolf shifter having two mates, but he couldn't focus, could barely think because he was looking at Dean. *Really* looking at him for the first time, but also as if he were staring at his oldest friend, someone he'd known his entire life.

Dean's gray eyes were glassy, reminding Luke of the ocean just after a storm, but he smiled through the tears threatening to spill. It was a nice smile. A really nice fucking smile. A really, *really* nice fucking smile. Luke's jaw actually went slack at the sight. Dean was practically glowing, the joy and relief lighting him up from within. Luke's eyes darted downwards without his permission. Apparently the phrase *built like a god* applied to demigods as well. Dean evidently had only been half-joking when he said Adonis looked like Quasimodo next to him.

Jesus. Fucking. Christ.

Luke had been attracted to males in the past, but had never moved past harmless flirting in bars. He felt his cheeks heat and forced all errant thoughts away, even as he again let his gaze brush over Dean's muscled chest and flat stomach, the dips and ridges of his abs, the fucking indentions beside his hips that Luke, himself, had and had been complimented on many times, but was only just now truly appreciating for the first time...

Dean surged forward and threw his arms around Luke, squeezing him so hard Luke couldn't breathe for a second, but he didn't mind. His eyes slid shut and Dean slapped him hard on the back. Luke returned the embrace, trying to ignore the clamoring and confusing instincts flaring, the intense emotions he was feeling. They shifted slightly and Dean stumbled.

"Fuck," Dean said pulling back and wiping at his eyes. "Not used to being on two legs it seems." He grinned and his eyes glittered with a casual, cocky mischief that made Luke smile in return. Despite everything, this was still Dean, still one of his closest friends, still one of the only people who truly seemed to *get* him to his very foundation.

"Some demigod, can't even walk," Luke said through the lump in his throat.

Dean grinned wider and punched Luke playfully in the shoulder. There was nothing in the touch except brotherly affection, like teammates messing around in the locker room before a game, and Luke's heart clenched. *Fuck.* He realized then that if—and that was a big *if* —Dean somehow *was* his, that didn't mean that Dean would feel the same. Mates were tricky when they were of different species, so fuck all when one of them was a godly being and the other a fucking *demigod.* These were uncharted waters and Luke was drowning. He told himself not to think about it right now, to just enjoy the moment, the fact that they'd actually succeeded and that Dean was no longer cursed, and he would figure out the rest later.

"I can't believe it," Dean whispered a bit hoarsely before clearing his throat. Luke wondered if his voice was always this husky or if it was just due to not using it in five hundred years. He had a slight accent, British-esque, though not quite. But whatever it was, it was extremely attractive and entirely unfair.

"We need to go," Emmie said. "Luke, help me."

Luke left Dean leaning against the wall and helped Sabina off of the floor to settle on the dirty cot in the corner. Sabina looked on the verge of passing out and Luke stepped away. Emmie moved forward and tucked a lock of tangled hair behind Sabina's ear. The Enchantress seemed to be forcing her eyes to remain open, and she sounded exhausted when she spoke.

"There's another exit from the dungeons, past my cell. Not many of the guards know of it and it leads to an abandoned outpost building near the edge of the compound."

"How do you know about it?" Luke asked skeptically, though he supposed she had absolutely no reason to lie to them.

"One of the guards uses it to slip out when he's supposed to be on night watch and fuck some cook. He likes to brag to me about how smart he was to discover it, trying to curry favor with Valen I suppose. You should be able to use it to get in and out unnoticed." Emmie nodded and began to ease away but Sabina grabbed her wrist. "Please come back for me. *Please*," she begged, eyes wide and beguiling.

"We will, I swear. Everything is coming together. You're going to play a big role in what's to come." Emmie winked at Sabina's confused expression, but the Enchantress' eyes slid closed and her body went limp, her chest rising and falling slowly.

Luke cut his gaze to Dean. He was leaning heavily against the door to the cell, looking like he might fall over as well. Luke bolted to his side and ducked his shoulder, draping Dean's arm over it. He wrapped his arm around Dean's back, supporting his weight. He mostly ignored the heat of Dean's body, the way they fit together. Mostly. Alright, not fucking at all. Luke ground his teeth and shook himself. He needed to get his shit together.

Dean exhaled roughly. "It's fine I can—"

"Oh shut up and come on," Luke interrupted. Dean gave in and leaned heavily on Luke, and the three of them made their way out of the dungeon, leaving the Enchantress Queen asleep in her cell.

TWELVE

He was himself again. Dean could hardly believe it was real. He kept half expecting to wake up from this dream and find himself as he'd been for the last five hundred years: furry and adorable and so pissed at the world he could burn the whole fucking thing down.

But, no. This was real. He was truly free of his curse. Once they'd cleared the compound and made it through the pass, he was feeling much more like a man again and his body had found its rhythms. He could walk again without help and with each step he felt stronger and stronger, his power and vitality flowing through his veins.

"Why do you keep looking at me like that?" he asked Luke as they walked through the woods back towards their secret clearing. Luke was on his right, glancing at him sidelong every few minutes, and Emmie was on his left gripping his hand. Luke's jaw had clenched at the sight of their clasped hands, but he'd otherwise shown no signs of irritation over it. Dean suspected that Luke assumed Emmie would choose Dean over him and had resigned himself to that fact, but Dean wasn't so sure—about the decision or the fact that it was that simple. He had a feeling things could get very complicated very quickly, but he was trying not to worry about it right now. He just wanted to revel in the fact that he was finally *free*. That he could finally touch Emmie; that he could embrace Luke or fight beside him if it came to that; that he could have a real conversation with them both on eye level like a man.

Luke started. "Like what?" he asked, clearing his throat.

"I don't know, like you expect me to sprout wings or shoot firebolts out of my eyes any second."

The tense set to Luke's shoulders relaxed a bit and he smiled that crooked, easy smile that Dean knew damn well could melt the panties off of any woman in a three-mile radius and make any man stop and stare.

"Maybe I do. I haven't exactly been around many demigods you know. I have no idea what to expect from you now that you aren't fuzzy wuzzy." He said the last bit in one of those voices you'd use when talking to an actual kitten and Dean scowled at him, which only made Luke smile bigger.

"No wings. No firebolts" Dean pursed his lips. "Well, not *exactly*." Luke's brows shot upward in interest. "My eyes turn gold with heightened emotion, like in the heat of battle say, and small flames run under my skin. I can sort of...will them into my blades."

"Whoa," Luke breathed. "So, you can fight with literal swords of fire?" Dean nodded. "Like Skylar. That's pretty badass, I'll give you that."

"I'm nowhere near as badass as that fearsome little creature," Dean admitted easily. It was true. He was nothing compared to a half-phoenix in her full glory, but, he wasn't a complete slouch either.

They continued to walk and Luke glanced at Dean again from the corner of his eye, as if he didn't want to be caught staring. With his enhanced hearing, Dean could hear how Luke's heart sped up inside his chest and longed to know what that was about. Was he thinking about losing Emmie again? Was he upset? Dean knew that the three of them would need to have an important talk at some point, but now was not the time.

Emmie stopped dead and tilted her head, her brows furrowed. She turned to look at Dean with a contemplative look on her beautiful face. Gods, has she always been so gorgeous? Dean was trying and failing to keep his thoughts from the proverbial gutter, but fuck it was hard—pun intended. He was hard as stone just from holding Emmie's hand, from looking at the way her pulse beat at the base of her slender, delicate throat, from imagining kissing her there, of touching her after so fucking long...

He cleared his throat now, realizing that she'd said something to him while his mind had been wandering.

"I'm sorry, what did you say, love?"

"I said, try to phase us back to the house."

His brows drew down and he actually huffed out a laugh when he realized that Luke wore an identical expression.

"But phasing doesn't work here...Ok, ok, don't give me that look," he added quickly when she narrowed her eyes, telling him in no uncertain terms to shut up and do what she said.

He reached out and clamped a hand on each of their shoulders and closed his eyes, fully expecting nothing to happen, but the familiar sensation of phasing settled over him like a warm blanket and a second later, he blinked open his eyes in front of the house.

"Holy shit," he breathed. "But how?"

Emmie grinned. "I have no idea. I just caught a glimpse of a vision of you phasing here and knew that it must work for you for some reason."

"Well, that will make getting back from this temple a bit easier at least," Luke said, shouldering open the front door.

Emmie and Dean followed him inside. The fireplaces and lights all flared to life and warmth enveloped them immediately, seeping into Dean's bones in a way he couldn't explain. It was like he'd been cold for five hundred years and had never realized it until this moment. Now, he was finally warm again, finally full of life and the absolute joy he felt was chasing away that cold, empty feeling that had settled into every inch of him while he'd been cursed.

Dean let his head fall back and his eyes slid closed, simply enjoying standing in a room, surrounded by warmth and people he... cared about. Deeply. So fucking deeply, it was a little terrifying and a lot confusing.

"How about a bath?" Emmie asked softly. "And a drink. A really, really big one."

Dean sighed roughly and opened his eyes. They met Emmie's and the fire in his chest blazed nearly out of control. He saw his eyes change in the reflection of her own, gold overtaking the gray and seeming to churn like liquid.

Luke cleared his throat quietly. "I'm going to go hunt. I'll be back."

"Luke, wait—" Dean called, but he'd already gone, the door slamming shut behind him.

"Come on, you," Emmie said, quietly. "He'll be alright, I promise." Emmie clasped Dean's hand and tugged him up the stairs towards the oversized master suite. The house somehow seemed to be bigger on the inside than it appeared on the outside, but Dean didn't question it, just followed Emmie obediently through the room and into the attached bathroom. She fiddled with the knobs and the huge tub—fuck, it was more like a small pool than a bathtub, really. Big enough to fit six people easily—began to fill with water, steam lazily filling the space with the scent of something floral and spicy.

Emmie ran her palm down Dean's chest and his entire body shuddered in response, each simple touch amplified by a thousand, a million. It was nearly painful, feeling her hands on him after so long. Each sensation was like an electric shock to his system, the most pleasurable pain he'd ever experienced.

"Go ahead and get in. I'm going to grab you that drink," she said softly before moving past him and out the door. He exhaled roughly and, despite his desperate need to touch her, to have her touch him and never stop, the bath did beckon. He quickly stepped out of his pants and tossed them aside, climbing over the wide edge of the stone tub and sinking in with a long, low moan. It was *glorious*. He'd forgotten what even the most simplistic sensations felt like, and each new one was like slowly taking one more step out of a dream. The hot water sliding over his skin, the soft abrasion of the sponge, the slick feel of the soap, his nails against his scalp as he shampooed his hair. Each new feeling brought him back to life, one step closer to being himself again.

Submerged benches ran along the edge of the tub, and Dean settled on one, leaning back against the smooth stone. He spread his arms out beside him, resting them on the edge of the tub, and let his head loll back. He felt more relaxed now than he had in almost too long to remember. He let himself just *be* for long moments, let everything that had happened wash over him. He let some things go, and others he held tighter to, vowing to never let them slip through his grasp again. He understood the irony of an immortal having a *life's too short* moment, but he didn't care. He understood all too well now how important things like love and friendship and not squandering the time you're given were.

He nearly jumped out of his skin when he heard the faint splash just across the tub. His eyes flashed open and Emmie was there, gliding slowly towards him. Her hair was pinned on top of her head in a messy knot, soft tendrils escaping and already sticking to her temples and neck from the steam. The water was just above her breasts, the oils and steam making it difficult to see beneath the surface.

Difficult, but not impossible.

He swallowed hard and his entire body went rigid as she neared. Her eyes were already darkening, the lavender shifting to a deep purple so dark it was nearly black, her runes glittering faintly in the low light. When had she turned the lights down...and where the fuck had all these candles come from? He glanced around briefly and found that the entire room was full of them. Hundreds probably. How lost in thought had he been?

She held out a glass when she was close enough that he could feel the heat from her body and he locked his muscles in place. He knew that Emmie wasn't fragile, knew that she was more powerful than he could ever hope to be, but still, he tried to tell himself to be careful. Not just physically. He knew that things were...complicated at the moment. He knew that she had feelings for Lucas. And fuck, so did he.

But he loved Emmie more than almost anything in all of the worlds, had for far too long. He had no fucking clue how to navigate all of this shit, but at the moment, all he could seem to see or hear or think about was Emmie. Emmie, who had been his friend and confidant and fellow-scoundrel and mischief-maker. Emmie, who had always come to him when he needed her most. Emmie, who had saved his life time and time again. Emmie, who he loved fiercely and without question or expectation.

His control was hanging on by a thread and it was unraveling by the second. He managed to reach out and take the glass with shaking hands, downing whatever was inside in one long gulp. He barely registered the burn, though a part of his mind appreciated the familiar warmth spreading through his chest. She eased forward without a word and draped herself over his lap, knees on either side of his hips. He reached up to cup her face with one big hand, brushing his thumb lightly across her cheekbone before leaning in to kiss her. Their lips met and an explosion of sensation rocked through him, making him gasp loudly against her mouth.

It was pleasure. It was pain. It was ecstasy.

Her lips were soft and warm against his, and despite the fact that he'd been dreaming of this moment for nearly five hundred years, he somehow kept things slow, appreciating and savoring every second, every breath, every heartbeat.

"Emmie," he whispered against her mouth, the word coming out like a benediction. She shuddered and he felt something warm and wet slide across his knuckles where he still held her face gently. He pulled back and saw the quicksilver tears tracking slowly down her face. He wiped one away with his thumb, leaving a streak of shimmering silver behind. "Shhh, it's ok, love."

"I missed you," she whispered. His chest constricted and he leaned in and kissed her cheek, erasing another tear with his lips. He kissed her other cheek, and then her eyelids, and forehead, and each corner of her mouth.

"I'm here now," he said roughly, the sting of tears burning his own eyes. She exhaled, long and low, and the weight of it made it seem as if she were releasing a breath she'd been holding for eons. She leaned in to kiss him again, wrapping her hands around the back of his neck and holding him to her. Her breasts pressed against his chest, her jutting nipples brushing against his skin and making his mouth water, and he could feel the beat of her heart, racing in time with his own. He wrapped his arms around her back, running his fingers along her shoulders and down her spine, wanting to touch every inch of her glorious body. He settled his hands on her hips as his tongue thrust gently against hers. Over and over, they explored and learned and remembered the way of each other.

She began to rock her hips, sliding over his aching cock. Gods, he was going to lose it like a teenage mortal, he just knew it. He had a fairly good excuse—it had been hundreds of years after all—but still. He called on every ounce of strength he possessed, determined to make this last as long as he possibly could.

He slid one hand between them and she quickly widened her knees, giving him the access he wanted so desperately he thought he might die. He ran his fingers over her, between her folds, making her moan quietly against his lips, before pressing a finger inside. He made some ridiculously embarrassing sound that was part groan, part moan, part growl.

So fucking hot. So fucking slick. So fucking mine.

He'd known it for so long but here, now, finally touching her like this, finally being with her this way, the knowledge ripped through him like a bolt of lightning. And yet...other knowledge shimmered around the edges, knowledge that it wasn't *just* Emmie for him...

He let those thoughts go for the moment though as Emmie writhed on top of him, riding his finger as he thrust it slowly before adding a second. Her nails dug into his shoulders and her runes glowed a shimmering silver, reflecting off of the water and making Dean feel as if they were floating high in a star-strewn sky.

"Dean," she whispered, begging. He couldn't hold back any longer. He removed his fingers and gripped his cock, positioning it just below her. She pulled back to meet his gaze as she slid downward.

"*Fuuucckkk,*" he groaned. Gods the feel of her, hot and wet around him, tight as a fist. It was paradise. It was euphoria. It was what he'd been waiting an eternity for. Her eyes were nearly black but the lavender ring flared brightly as she held his gaze. The pleasure and desire and love all flashing within the endless depths made his chest twist. He held her stare, biting down on his lower lip so hard he nearly drew blood in an effort to keep himself from moving an inch, from breaking this impossibly perfect moment.

When he was seated inside her as far as he could go, she stilled, letting her body adjust and giving them both a moment to fully comprehend what was happening, to savor what they'd both been waiting so long for, for what Dean hadn't been certain he'd ever have. He reached out and tucked a lock of silvery hair behind her ear before caressing her cheek.

"So long," he whispered hoarsely, "I've been waiting so long, Em."

She covered his hand with her own, eyes sliding closed as she leaned into his touch. And then she started to move, sliding up until she was barely seated on the end of his cock before gliding back downward. They both moaned quietly as she repeated the motion over and over. Slow. Languid. Savoring. There would be a time when he would wrench her down on his cock, when he would take her from behind until she screamed with pleasure, when he would fuck her against a wall without abandon, using all the power they both possessed, the power they could both handle, until neither one of them could walk, or move, or speak, or think. There would be a time for all of that.

But now was not that time.

Now, it was more than sex. It was so much more than anything he could possibly explain. She opened her eyes and held his gaze as she rode him in a slow rhythm, conveying with her body and her eyes everything that she felt, everything that mirrored what he felt to the depths of his soul. He slid his hand to her clit and slowly massaged, applying gentle pressure in time with her movements.

"Ah, gods," she moaned. "Don't stop. Please don't stop."

He didn't. He couldn't. He arched his hips upward as she slid downward, enough to get deeper, but still keeping things slow. He leaned forward and kissed her, brushing his tongue against hers in long, sweeping thrusts. She sucked gently on his lower lip and he nearly growled. Gods, it was too much. Everything was too much. It had been too long. Each touch, each lick, each stroke, was like a jolt through his entire body, like he was touching one of those electric fences that mortals used to keep livestock from running wild.

"Better stop that, love," he whispered against her lips and felt her grin. He couldn't help smiling back but he thrust his hips a little harder this time, making her grin fade and a gasp escape her lips. Water splashed over the edge of the tub as they moved, losing themselves in each other. He rubbed her clit harder, and her thighs began to shake around his hips.

"Better *not* stop that," she said, breathless. He barked out a laugh and continued, gripping her hip with one hand to guide her thrusts. "Oh gods, right there. *Righttthererighttthererighttthere.* I'm going to... come..."

With one more thrust of his hips upward, she threw her head back and screamed as she came hard around him. Her runes flared so brightly they were nearly blinding. He could feel her, could feel the tight pulses as her orgasm rocked through her and he knew he was done for. He felt the tightening in his spine that he hadn't experienced in so damn long, the climbing, climbing, climbing...

"*FUCK!*" he roared as he came so hard the entire room seemed to shake around them. Flames sprang to life across his skin, dancing down his arms and across his chest. They couldn't harm another person unless they were pushed into a blade, so he had no fear for Emmie's safety, but he rarely lost control of his power like this. *It's been five hundred years. Give yourself a break.*

After a few more moments, Emmie collapsed against his chest, limp and shuddering lightly.

"Fucking hell," he whispered, voice hoarse.

"As good as you remember?" she asked, panting, but he could hear the smile in her voice.

"I have no recollection of sex before this moment," he told her honestly. This had been unlike anything he'd ever experienced in all of his long life. He'd fucked more times than he could hope to count, but this was something so different. Something more.

Dean gently stroked her spine while they both caught their breath and his mind wandered a bit. Luke's face floated into his thoughts and he stiffened.

"What? What's wrong?" she asked, sitting back to stare at him.

"I..." He ran a hand through his damp hair and exhaled roughly. "Luke," he finally said. "He's in love with you, I don't want him hurt."

She eyed him suspiciously and he could see in her eyes that she knew, could see the words she was choosing not say: *You're in love with him too.* She was going to let him deal with that when he was ready, which was not this moment.

"It's...complicated, yes," she said, using his words from before and reaching out to run her fingers across his jaw, his cheek, his brow, as if she wanted to touch every inch of him, as if she needed to keep touching him to convince herself that it was real, that he was truly himself again. "But everything will be ok. Or well, that's a very loaded statement," she amended. "Big bad coming down on us all soon and I don't know the outcome yet...but with us? The three of us? Things will work out the way they're supposed to."

He had no idea what that actually meant, but before he could press for more clarification or push away the empty feeling in his chest, the place that belonged to Luke, he knew, Emmie scrunched her nose and grinned.

"Let's get you cleaned up. You smell like a wet cat."

THIRTEEN

Things were...tense between the three of them, though no one seemed ready or willing to address the giant fucking elephant in the room.

Lucas had run for *hours* the night Dean's curse had been lifted. He'd told himself he was doing the noble thing in giving Dean and Emmie time together. Time they deserved, of course, and time that Luke was happy for them to have after everything they'd both been through.

But it was also time that was ripping Luke's insides to shreds as if he'd swallowed razor blades dipped in acid. Even as he felt joy for their joy, wanting two people he...cared for so much to be happy, he felt sick with jealousy, and fear, and loss. A loss so profound he could barely comprehend it.

So, he did the only thing he could think to do and ran. He ran and ran and ran, desperate for the feel of the earth beneath his paws and the wind in his fur to ease his mind, to erase all thoughts, to dull the edges of the pain. He'd finally come to the edge of a lake, dark, boiling water swirling beneath the jagged cliff. He'd changed back into his human form and screamed. He'd screamed until his throat was raw and his voice was hoarse. Then, he finally collapsed to his knees and let the misery wash over him.

When he'd returned to the house who knows how long later, Dean had been standing in the kitchen, drinking water. His eyes widened when he took in Luke. Sweaty, dirty, features hardened to keep the pain from showing. The people he worked with had always joked that he was a robot because he was so adept at hiding his emotions behind a bored, unaffected façade. He was thankful for it in that moment. He didn't need Dean pitying him or trying to console him.

"Are you alright?" Dean asked, staring at Luke intently.

"Fine," he'd said a little gruffly before clearing his throat. Neither one of them seemed to know what to say, so they just stood for a long moment. "I need to shower," Luke finally said, and headed towards the hallway that led to one of the bedrooms on the lower floor.

"Luke, wait," Dean called out.

Luke stopped and turned, holding up a hand.

"It's ok, you don't have to..." He closed his eyes and shook his head. "It's ok," he said again, his shoulders slumping a bit. "I'm happy for you, for you both, really, I am. I knew...I knew when we started this trip that I only had so much time left with her, that once you were back things would be different."

"Luke," Dean said again, brows drawn and his handsome features screwed up in something that looked a mix of confusion and pain.

"I'll see you in the morning." Luke strode away before Dean could say another word, ducking into the room and closing the door behind him.

In the days that followed while they rested and planned, things had been...weird. But also not weird at the same time, which was even weirder. It still felt so normal and right for the three of them to be together, just like it had before Dean had been changed, back when they'd spent countless nights doing research or watching TV or playing Xbox.

But beneath the normalcy, was the fucking tension.

Tension because no one had come out and said that Dean and Emmie were officially together, though that was the case...wasn't it? Tension because she still gave Luke heated glances, still reached for his hand sometimes when they were walking or standing near each other. Tension because Luke couldn't stop noticing Dean, the way his body moved, the way he laughed, the way his gray eyes lit with amusement and mischief...

Tension because Emmie was slipping into his bedroom at this very moment.

Luke had been lying on the bed, staring up at the ceiling with his hands behind his head, thinking about everything and trying to unravel the mystery of his confusing instincts and feelings, when the door creaked open. He shot upwards, eyes widening when he saw Emmie closing the door behind her, a look on her face that he couldn't quite decipher. Determined. Desirous. Sexy.

"Are you alright? Is something wrong?" Luke asked quietly, body going tense.

"Nothing's wrong," she whispered, gliding towards the bed, hips swaying in a sultry rhythm that made him feel as if he were being hypnotized. He didn't move as she made her way over; didn't move as she wordlessly reached down and untied the thin robe she was wearing, letting the silk pool on the floor around her feet, and making his heart thunder and his mouth go dry at the sight of her gloriously naked before him save a tiny excuse for a thong; didn't move as she crawled on hands and knees up the bed towards him.

"Emmie?" he choked when he finally found his voice again. "What..." She leaned in and kissed him, silencing the question. His eyes slid closed at the feel of her lips on his, the utter contentment and feeling of rightness washing over him like a wave. He cupped her face, fingertips gliding into the edges of her silky hair as she deepened the kiss, her breasts brushing against his bare chest and making him shudder. He nearly lost himself in the kiss, but confusion won out over lust—barely.

"Wait, wait, wait," he said, pulling away. "I don't understand. I thought...with Dean back..."

"I love you too, Luke. You have to know that," she said quietly, holding his gaze. He saw nothing but truth there, the power of the words slamming into him and making him nearly gasp. *She loves me.* "Dean being back doesn't change that."

"But..." His mind was whirling. He didn't understand what this meant, what was happening, how to reconcile all of the information in a way that made any kind of sense.

"Luke, stop overthinking. I can smell the burning rubber." She grinned and he barked out a stunned laugh. "Do you love me?" she asked, gaze serious and oddly vulnerable. Could she possibly not *know?*

"Yes," he said. "Yes, I do. You're mine, Emmie. I've known it for months..." There was so much more to say, so much more confusion to add, but he stopped the thoughts as she leaned forward again and kissed him. He loved her and she loved him and things were complicated and confusing as all fuck, but he didn't care. Right now, he just wanted her. He wanted to forget everything outside of this room and just be with the woman that he loved, the woman that had been given to him by fate.

She moved to straddle his hips, running her hands over his chest and down his stomach. His muscles clenched in response, her touch setting him on fire. He grabbed her waist, fingers digging in, but he quickly loosened his grip. She made a sound of annoyance.

"I won't break, Luke," she whispered, biting his lower lip just hard enough, just how he liked. His cock jumped in response and she moaned softly, rocking her hips. He gripped her tightly again, and pulled her hard against him, thrusting his hips upward as he did and making her gasp. Her nails dug into the back of his head as he thrust his tongue against hers harder, dominating her mouth. Instincts flared, practically screaming in his head: *Dominate. Bite. Claim.*

As if she could hear it, Emmie rasped, "Claim me, Luke." Part of him wanted to argue, to say that he couldn't claim her when he didn't know if she was actually *his*, if she would actually be with him, but that part was drowned out by the rest, the part that was already spinning them so that she was pinned beneath him. She gasped in surprise, but the gasp quickly transformed into a moan as he ground his hips against her while he palmed her breast, brushing his thumb over her nipple and making her shudder.

"Oh gods," she rasped, back bowing off of the bed. Her hands were suddenly in his sweatpants, gripping his cock with soft, warm fingers. He gnashed his teeth, teeth that were already lengthening and sharpening. He swiped at the flimsy strings holding her panties on her hips with a claw, and the material fell away as if it were made of smoke. He made sure they were retracted before he reached down and quickly thrust two fingers deep inside her.

"Ohhhhh," she moaned, writhing, digging her heels into the mattress and bucking her hips upward, begging for more.

"So fucking hot," he groaned. "So slick and tight, Emmie. *Fuck*."

"Gods I love the way you talk," she panted.

"And I love the way you feel. The way you taste." She whimpered as he bent his head and took her nipple into his mouth, sucking hard as he thrust his fingers over and over. He would normally make her wait to come, drawing out the pleasure longer, but not tonight. Need was riding him harder than ever before. The need to bury himself inside her. The need to bite her, to claim her, to make her his. So, he curled his fingers, hitting just the right spot, pressed his thumb against her clit, and flicked his tongue over her nipple.

"Luke!" she yelled, fingers threading through his hair and holding his head to her breast. Lights flared beneath her skin, her tattoos glowing as she came in a rush, quick and hard. He could feel her pussy clenching his fingers but he forced himself to pull them away. She made an adorable whining noise, but bit her lip and watched him raptly, eyes nearly black, as he put his fingers in his mouth, sucking and groaning in bliss. "*Fuck*," she whispered, breathless, eyes wide. "Such a dirty little wolf, aren't you?" Her eyes glittered in the darkness and the look set him on fire.

He quickly yanked his pants and briefs off. She pushed up on her elbows to stare at him, the lavender ring in her eyes burning brightly. He arched a brow, letting her look, loving the feel of her eyes on him. He gripped his cock, stroking himself as she watched, and her breaths shallowed, her chest rising and falling in quick bursts.

"I could watch you do that all night," she rasped, running her tongue over her bottom lip.

"And one day, I'll let you. But right now...Fuck, Emmie, I need to..." He ground his teeth, fighting to keep control. "I don't know that I can be...easy," he hedged. No, he couldn't be easy. He needed to fuck her hard, to make her scream into oblivion, to mark her in all ways as his own.

"I don't want easy," she said, giving him a challenging look. Luke's cock jerked at that, desperate to slam inside her. A very small part of his mind wondered if Dean could hear everything that was happening, if he cared, if he was jealous.

"Then turn over," he said gruffly. Her eyes widened and she inhaled sharply, but she did as he asked, rising up on her hands and knees before him. He knelt on the bed behind her, reaching out to run a hand over her perfect ass, kneading as he stroked his shaft with his other hand. She whimpered, wiggling her ass as if begging him to continue. A low growl rumbled from his chest. Fuck, she was perfect.

Mine.

Unable to wait any longer, he nudged her legs apart with his knees and she panted in anticipation. Though he was nearly out of his mind with desperate, frenzied desire, he took a heartbeat to admire the view.

"Fucking hell, Emmie," he gasped. With her ass in the air, legs spread, and pussy dripping, he nearly came at the sight. He moved forward and positioned his cock, hissing when the head dipped inside and met wet heat. "Ready?" he bit out with some effort.

"Do it, Luke. *Please.*" She shifted backwards and he slid inside the tiniest bit.

Fuck. Me.

That was it, his control snapped like a rubber band pulled too tight. He shoved his hips forward, surging inside her and making her cry out. He gripped her hips, holding her in place and stilled, sweat beading on his forehead. "Alright?" he ground out. He was afraid he'd hurt her, but then he realized her cry was of pure pleasure, wet heat surrounding his shaft and her fingers digging into the sheets as she moaned and arched her back.

"More!" she demanded. It was all he needed to hear. He shifted his hips backwards and slammed forward again, holding her hips steady as he fucked her hard, over and over. Her breasts bounced as he thrust forward, the sounds of her screams and his groans and grunts and growls filling the space around them.

"That's right, Em. Gods, you take me so fucking well. Look at you, sweetheart…"

"Oh my gods," Emmie hissed. "Harder. Keep talking. *Fuckfuck-fuck.*" She sounded nearly out of her mind and he fucking loved it.

Her wish was his command. He wound her long hair around his fist and tugged her head back, pushing her shoulders down with the other hand. He pinned her there, lifting her ass higher and slamming hard inside her, getting deeper with the slightly different angle. "FUCK!" she yelled. "Yes, just like that! Oh Gods, Luke…"

They were both slick with sweat when his fangs throbbed so hard that he couldn't ignore them any longer, his instincts demanding that he claim her. He pulled her up against his chest, still on his knees and still thrusting his hips. He brushed her hair away, baring the vulnerable spot where her neck met her shoulder. He snaked one hand around and rubbed her clit and she moaned loudly, head resting trustingly against his chest.

"Going to…bite you…" he growled.

"*Yes,*" she panted, nearly mindless.

He took a heartbeat to fully appreciate what was happening, the fact that he was about to claim his mate, and in that precious, endless moment, Dean's face flashed behind his eyes, there and gone in an instant. Before he could think too much about that, Luke lowered his head and sank his fangs into Emmie's flesh.

She screamed out, but not in pain. Oh no. She came *instantly*, pussy walls clenching him with the thrashing waves of her climax. Her flesh gloved his fangs, his instincts roaring with triumph. She reached back and dug her fingers in his hair, holding him to her. She *liked* his bite. She *liked* being claimed.

He quickly followed her over the edge, roaring against her neck as he came, hot and deep inside her. He held her tight against his chest as they collapsed into a puddle on the mattress. He withdrew his fangs and wiped away the small trickle of blood that oozed from the puncture marks. They were already closing with her enhanced healing, but he could still see them. Any shifter would be able to forever, would know that she was claimed, that she was *his*.

Their breaths were loud in his ears, their hearts both thundering, but he felt such an utter contentment that a tightness in his chest that he hadn't even known was there suddenly relaxed. He'd loved Skylar, but knew she wasn't his. He'd had fun with Zahara, both of them finding release and escape with each other over the years. But nothing had ever felt like this. It was like a piece of himself had been missing all this time and it was finally back where it belonged, clicking loudly into place.

But he wasn't completely whole. Not yet.

He was too exhausted to figure out what that was about. He eased out of Emmie, managed to stumble to the bathroom and grab a towel to clean them both up. He stretched out behind her and pulled an already-nearly-comatose Emmie back against his chest, kissing the top of her head, and muttering "I love you" before he passed out cold.

FOURTEEN

The three of them were all acting totally normal, as if Dean hadn't slept with Emmie, and as if she hadn't slept with Luke, and as if Dean wasn't *also* dying to sleep with Luke but refusing to say anything.

Yep, totally fucking normal.

They'd avoided talking about the things they obviously needed to talk about by focusing on the admittedly more important task of getting Sabina's amulet so they could get the fuck out of here and go home. Emmie was getting anxious, talking about running out of time and needing to get the pieces to their proper positions on the board. So, they'd hiked for nearly two days straight in order to reach the temple high up in the mountains. Dean could have potentially phased them up the mountainside as far as he could see, but without knowing what kind of security measures or guards were in place, it was too risky.

So, they'd hiked and avoided conversations that they should probably have. Not that Dean knew what the hell he would even say if someone *did* want to talk about it. He could no less give up Emmie than he could give up breathing, but Emmie was Luke's mate. There was no way *he* could give her up either.

So...did they share? It wasn't unheard of, especially among the gods, but there was an extra layer of confusion thrown in: Dean was in love with Luke too. He wasn't sure how he would handle an eternity of unrequited love when the object of his affection was constantly there in front of him, happily in love with someone else two feet away.

Complicated was an understatement, so Dean tried to force the thoughts away and focus on the mission.

They'd made it up the mountain and to the temple without encountering much of anything, but the temple itself was a different story. It had been far more fortified than they could have imagined, layer upon layer of protection, like the world's deadliest obstacle course. They'd fought through a garden maze full of man-eating plants with thorns the size of daggers, made it across an expansive courtyard where each wrong step sent poison-tipped arrows flying their direction, and barely survived traversing the open-air atrium where geysers of lava erupted from the ponds all around them.

And that was all just the outer grounds of the damn place.

When they finally made it inside the actual temple, a gigantic stone edifice built right into the side of the mountain, they braced for the worst, but...nothing happened. No arrows, no lava, no pits of vipers. Nada.

Dean met Emmie and Luke's eyes and shrugged, and they all made their way cautiously forward through the foyer-type area with a high domed ceiling. Dean supposed it was a narthex since this was technically a church of sorts. A wide, spiraling staircase sat on the other side. No other doors or hallways seemed to branch off the main space.

"Up it is?" Emmie asked. Dean and Luke shared a look before nodding. They cautiously made their way across the wide room, eyes darting constantly, ready and alert and expecting the worse. But again, nothing happened. Dean gestured for them to stop, taking a tentative step up onto the first stair. He shrugged and they all slowly headed up the stairs.

"Maybe we passed all the hard stuff," Emmie said casually.

"Oh, right. It'll just be smooth sailing from here on out. We'll just waltz right in and—"

Luke's words cut off in a yell as the entire staircase collapsed under their feet. Emmie screamed and they plummeted towards the stone floor below...only for it to open up at the last second, like a trap door. They tumbled to the ground about twenty feet down, falling together in a heavy thud of tangled limbs and grunts. Nothing immediately came out of the woodworks, so they lay there for a few seconds catching their breaths and recovering.

"It's raining...cats...and dogs," Emmie panted.

Luke groaned and Dean covered his face with his hands. "You did not just say that..."

"I've been waiting a thousand years to make that joke. I never could quite figure out when or where it was happening, but I've been sitting on that one for a millennia."

Luke rolled over and untangled himself from Dean and Emmie's sprawled limbs.

"Just because you've been sitting on the joke for a thousand years, does not mean it's a good one."

"I beg to differ," she pouted.

"No, love, he's right. That was terrible," Dean said with a half-smile, rubbing his ribs and wincing. At least one of them was cracked, maybe two. He ignored the pain and gave Emmie a concerned look. "Are you sure this temple is only affecting your powers? Not your mental faculties as well? Because if you really think that was a good joke, I am very, very concerned..."

"Har har. So funny." Her eyes flashed with annoyance but she seemed to be fighting a smile, despite how much Dean knew being powerless was bothering her. They had no idea why, but all of her powers started going on the fritz as soon as they'd stepped foot on what the Order deemed sacred ground. Another weird quirk of this realm, they guessed.

She had been trained in swordplay and combat by Hades, so Dean wasn't worried about her ability to defend herself, but he knew how naked she felt without her abilities. And not the good kind of naked. The kind he shouldn't be thinking about at the moment but couldn't quite make himself stop. Flashes of their time in the bath ran through his mind and he cleared his throat, heat creeping up the back of his neck.

"I really hate this gods' forsaken place," Emmie added in a grumble.

They all managed to make it to their feet and staggered towards a towering door made of gleaming red wood. They all silently agreed to take a little breather before going through since this area seemed relatively safe. After the initial fall through the floor, it had gone back to radio silence from all things trying to kill them.

Luke slid down to the dusty floor, leaning heavily against the stone wall. He tilted his head back and closed his eyes, and Dean eyed him critically, his chest clenching. Luke's face was coated in dried blood, his shirt ripped in several places, and his forearm was still covered with angry, blistered skin where lava had caught him. Nothing was fatal and he was already healing, but seeing Lucas injured didn't sit well with Dean.

"I'm fine," Luke said on an irritated exhale without opening his eyes, "stop staring at me." Emmie met Dean's eyes and her lips curled upward, but she gasped a moment later.

"I can feel it! The amulet. I can feel it's power. Sabina's power, I mean. We're close."

Luke pried his eyes open and he and Dean shared a look. It was a look that two warriors shared in battle when they didn't think they could continue, but knew that they somehow would, that they would draw strength from each other and find a way to make it through. Luke nodded and pushed up from the floor, taking another sip from his canteen before tucking it into one of the many pockets of his tactical pants. It was so the wrong time, but Dean couldn't help but notice how damn good Lucas looked in them. They hugged his narrow hips and powerful thighs, and the weapons belt slung around his waist just added to the appeal. A sword hung at his hip, all manner of other sharp implements of death attached all around within easy reach, though his body was a weapon more powerful than any of those. The tight black shirt he wore molded over his thick chest and muscled arms, his biceps straining the stretchy, but nearly impenetrable material.

"What?" Luke asked, sounding irritated.

Dean blinked and realized that he'd been staring. *Fuck.*

"You've got a little something right here. Wasn't sure if you knew," Dean teased, indicating the side of his own face. Luke rolled his eyes and swiped a hand over his cheek where he did, in fact, have a thick streak of dirt mixed with blood.

"Hilarious. Fucking hilarious," he muttered, rolling his eyes. He blew out a long breath and put his hand on the door. "Ready?"

Emmie nodded and Dean gave a customary swaggering grin, though he didn't really feel it.

"I'm always ready, pup."

Luke's lips curled upward on one side and he shook his head, laughing lightly despite himself.

"I liked you better when you were a cat."

"Words hurt, Lucas," Dean chided as he stepped up beside Luke and they shouldered open the door together, Emmie entering behind them.

"Sticks and stones may break my bones, but whips and chains excite me," Emmie sang quietly as they moved forward into the unknown.

"Be ready," Dean said quietly, sword at the ready. Emmie could feel the tension roiling off both of them in waves. She didn't blame them. If the amulet was here, then there was surely something guarding it, something worse than everything else they'd faced so far. Her heart had stopped beating too many times to count already, each time one of her boys had been injured or very nearly killed. She knew they had a lot to discuss, but first they needed to focus on getting out of this place alive. Then she'd gladly lay everything out on the table.

They were running out of time, both in terms of needing to get back to Aqueous to get Si and Beck all straightened out and those plans in motion, but also possibly just in general. Darkness was coming. Big, bad darkness, and of the millions of outcomes that had flashed through her mind, there was only one in which they came out victorious.

But winning didn't mean that they wouldn't lose people.

She pushed the thought away, not able to stomach the idea of losing anyone she loved, but especially not Dean or Lucas. She hadn't had time with them yet. After eons of waiting, she deserved time, damn it. So, she vowed that once they made it out of this—and she was certain they would, just not exactly how—they would stop pussy-footing around and talk about what was going on with the three of them. They would figure it the fuck out.

They slowly made their way forward, and Luke scanned the area, his dark eyes moving quickly over every shadow and recess, prepared for something to leap at them at any moment. The temple had been built right into a soaring peak of the mountain, and now they were in the heart of it. The signs of man—or goblin—made architecture had faded away now, becoming an enormous, natural cave. The rough stone walls around them soared so high that they disappeared into blackness overhead, and the ground beneath their feet was covered in loose dirt and rocks. It was illuminated by torches set within the rocks, but it was still dim. Thankfully a demigod, a shifter, and whatever the hell she was could all see perfectly fine in the dark.

"Emmie?" Dean asked.

"It's definitely here," she answered, eyes narrowed and unease prickling up her spine.

"Then why," Lucas asked cautiously, "haven't we been attacked yet?" Her thoughts exactly. She shared a look with Luke and then her gaze darted to Dean, her concern mirrored back in his gray eyes. They were halfway across the cave and *nothing* had happened yet. No booby traps. No poisoned arrows, or walls of fire, or big, giant, fearsome beasties. *So...what the fuck?*

"You know that's the worst possible thing you can say in this situation, don't you?" Dean groaned with a roll of his eyes as he strode a few feet away. "Like saying the words *perfect game* when the pitcher is on the verge of having one. You just don't do it, man. It's the ultimate jinx."

Luke took a few steps to Emmie's left, checking a small recess in the stone, and admitted, "Ok, you're right. My bad."

Emmie tilted her head as Dean began kicking at something on the ground.

"What is it?"

"Bones," the demigod answered, and then frowned. "Not that old, and..." He narrowed his eyes and bent down to look closer. "And...they look like they've been *gnawed* on."

"Gnawed? What the—"

Lucas broke off as the ground suddenly groaned and buckled beneath them. Emmie staggered, throwing out a hand to grab onto Luke just as a giant fissure opened just behind them across the center of the cave. Hunks of rock rained down all around them and Luke threw his arms over her, trying to shield her from the assault.

"Dean!" Luke yelled out, holding out a hand towards the demigod just as the ground beneath them surged upward, like a pillar rising out of the earth. Emmie screamed and Luke's arms clamped around her like a vice. He dropped to his knees and pulled her beneath him, using his body to shield her and take every blow. She could feel more than hear him grunt in pain as chunks of stone pelted him.

After what felt like an eternity, though she was sure it had only been a few seconds, the quaking of the earth all around them finally stopped. Luke pulled away and gripped her upper arms, searching her face and body quickly for injuries.

"Are you alright?" he asked urgently, his hands gently moving to cup her face.

She gripped his wrists and nodded. "I'm alright, Luke. I'm fine." Fresh blood ran down his temple where a rock had sliced his scalp, and she knew his back must have taken a beating as well, but before she could ask, he jumped to his feet and rushed to the edge of their pedestal of stone.

"Dean!" he yelled again, a frantic edge to his voice, and Emmie's own breath caught in her throat. He was a demigod, but they had no fucking clue what was down that crevice. It could be hellsfire; it could be pit filled with godsblades; it could be a portal to another realm where they might not have any hope of ever retrieving him.

"I'm here. I'm alright," he called from below. Luke's shoulders relaxed a fraction and Emmie blew out a relieved breath. "Are you both ok?"

Emmie edged forward cautiously, moving to stand beside Lucas and peer over the edge. The air was still thick with clouds of dust and dirt, but she could see Dean's outline. She glanced around as the dust finally began to settle and she saw that several other sections of rock had risen upward as well, seemingly at random.

Dean smiled up at them both, and though he was bloody and covered in dirt, it was a brilliant smile, one that made her heart speed up.

"We're fine. We—" Luke cut off as an unearthly roar echoed around them, so loud that the stone beneath their feet trembled again from the force of it and Emmie barely stopped herself from covering her ears.

"Oh *fuck*," Dean groaned as a gigantic beast emerged from a tunnel that had opened when all the rocks shifted. It stalked forward with a surprising agility and grace. It looked a bit like a giant lion, but more reptilian, with blue, iridescent scales covering its hide, slitted crimson eyes, and a spiked tail that flicked behind it like an angry cat's. Talons the size of small swords clicked against the loose pebbles as it eased forward, a low hissing-growl rumbling through its chest.

Dean backed up slowly, popping his sword off of the ground with his foot and catching it with one hand in one graceful, easy movement, and glanced around for an escape. Emmie did the same, desperate to haul his ass to safety, but something sparkling in the darkness behind the beast caught her eye. She reached out and grabbed Luke's arm, squeezing tightly.

"Luke," she breathed, and he yanked his head up to meet her eyes. He frowned and followed her gaze over his shoulder. He inhaled sharply when he saw it too, but before he could say anything, the monster roared again and their eyes both snapped back to Dean.

"Dean," Emmie warned, "mind the tail!" As if in response, the beast flicked its tail angrily and it smashed into the stone wall on their left, a shower of jagged rocks raining down. Its lips curled back from its teeth, and a green, viscous liquid dripped from its fangs. The ground sizzled and smoked where it struck, and Emmie swallowed hard. "And the acid-coated fangs, apparently."

"WHAT THE FUCK IS THIS THING??" Dean yelled as he backed away, keeping himself low and balanced.

"Looks like the bastard offspring of a dragon and some kind of big cat," Luke said, eyes searching the cave. He needed to figure this out. He needed to get Dean out of harm's way, keep Emmie safe, and get that fucking amulet, and he needed to do them all simultaneously and right fucking now.

Think, McBride. Think, think, think...

He came up with and discarded plan after plan, gritting his teeth in frustration. His instincts were screaming, pounding in his head and chest so forcefully he thought he might be ripped apart from the inside. He needed to protect them. It was his duty, his purpose in life, and he couldn't fail. He *wouldn't* fail.

"That was fucking rhetorical, pup!" Dean called back as he lunged to the left and barely escaped being gutted when the thing swiped a taloned paw in his direction. A heartbeat later, Dean's body began to...glow. No, not glow—*burn*. Flames licked down his arms and flowed into his sword, and for a moment, Luke was distracted. More than distracted. He was fucking *mesmerized*. Dean in battle, flaming sword at the ready like some sort of avenging angel, was something to behold. He moved like smoke, spinning and ducking and slashing out with a lethal grace that left Luke in absolute awe.

Even so, the beast was massive and lightning quick, and though Dean was landing blows that made the monster shriek and hiss in pain and rage, it wasn't enough. It didn't slow and it was backing Dean towards the chasm. The demigod glanced behind him, cursed, and darted to the side just as the beast slashed out again, but he wasn't fast enough. He cried out in pain as claws raked his side and Emmie screamed.

"I've gotta get down there," Luke said, fear clamping around his heart like a vice. He glanced around wildly, sizing up his options. Just as he was calculating the distance to a small ledge behind the beast, Dean's voice rang out.

"Don't even think about it, pup! You stay right the fuck there!" There was power and authority laced in his voice, and Luke realized that this wasn't the voice of the charismatic, cocky, playful friend he'd come to know and care for. No, this was the voice of a demigod warrior who commanded armies beside Ares. It was terrifying and awe-inspiring...and sort of hot. Ok, very hot. *So not the time, McBride,* Luke thought to himself with shake of his head.

"Stay. The fuck. There!" Dean ground out, punctuating each word with a slash of his sword. Black blood splattered the cave wall and the beast roared in pain and frustration. Luke knew he should do what Dean said, that he should stay and protect Emmie since she had no power here, but they had to get the amulet. It was the whole fucking point, their ticket out of here.

He turned to Emmie, quickly shucking off his weapons belt and fastening it around her waist and cinching it tight. He repeated Dean's words now: "Stay here."

"Luke, wait—"

He didn't wait. He turned and leapt off of the rock before he could think better of it, launching himself towards the wall of the cave. There was a small outcropping of rock just to the left of the tunnel the beast had come out of.

Very small.

Ok...maybe nonexistent, he thought as he flew closer, his enhanced eyesight realizing too late that what he thought was a ledge was an optical illusion, just shadows against the flat, rough wall.

"Oh fuck," he groaned just as he heard Dean's outraged roar. This was going to fucking hurt, but there was nothing to be done for it now. Luke turned just before he reached the rock, his wolf's claws extending and slamming into the wall. He bit back a yelp of pain as they dug into the stone, several of them ripping off completely and blood beginning to pour from the gaping wounds. He snarled and curled his lips away from his fangs, gnashing his teeth but refusing to give into the agony.

It worked. It slowed his decent downward enough that he could leap to the ground without breaking his legs. He held on for a moment longer, gnashing his teeth against the pain, and then let go, tumbling downward and nearly collapsing when he hit the ground in a jarring thud. But to his relief, nothing snapped or shattered, so he would call it a win.

He pushed onto shaking legs and the hair on the back of his neck rose just as Emmie and Dean both screamed his name. He spun and saw the beast, its massive jaws only a few feet away, its fangs spewing acrid smelling venom. *Fuck.* He hadn't planned on sliding down the fucking wall, hadn't planned on landing in a vulnerable heap on the floor like lunch served on a silver platter for this thing.

He'd fucked up. He tensed, prepared for whatever was about to happen, when a silvery streak flew in front of him.

Luke's eyes widened just as Dean yelled her name.

"EMMIE!" It was a mix of rage and utter terror and Luke's heart stopped beating completely as she slid on her knees below the beast's outstretched neck, just as it snapped its jaws towards Luke. Her sword sliced through the thick scales and blood poured as the beast reared back, shrieking.

Emmie yelled out in pain as the blood splattered her skin, burning on contact, but she gritted her teeth and leapt up.

"Go, Luke!" she yelled. "Get the fucking amulet!!"

He hesitated for a fraction of a second as she turned to face the beast again, Dean rushing forward from behind to help. Then he turned and sprinted down the tunnel, the dim, blue sparkle brightening as he got closer and closer. He finally reached the simple stone pedestal and changed back into this human form mid stride. He had no idea how his clothing always survived the change unscathed, but he was thankful for whatever mystical power allowed it for all shifters—he would have hated having to run around naked all the time, especially in the middle of a battle.

He skidded to a stop just before the pedestal and reached out to snatch the large sapphire pendant on the braided gold chain. He knew he should be more cautious, that there may be even more traps, but he couldn't make himself care. He needed this done and to get back to Emmie and Dean. His fingers closed around the stone, and he could feel the power within it pulse against his palm, hot and jolting, but nothing else happened. He exhaled and turned to sprint back towards the cave. His lips curled in triumph and his gaze locked with Emmie's when he was a few yards from the mouth of the tunnel. She smiled back but then her face crumbled, a scream rending the air, and Luke's entire body went rigid.

The beast had swiped out, its talons slicing at Emmie's back and she fell to her knees. Dean looked like a warrior angel, all gold and fire as he bellowed in utter rage and leapt higher than any being should be able to leap, straight onto the beast's back. He drove his sword of fire downward, directly through the beast's skull. Its scream only lasted for a moment before it collapsed, blood pouring from the wound like black lava when Dean yanked his sword out and jumped from its carcass, sprinting to Emmie. Luke closed the remaining distance between them in what felt like a heartbeat.

"What were you thinking?!" Dean demanded, voice choked. "Why did you leave the rock?" He gingerly inspected her back and she winced through clenched teeth.

"Dis...traction," she said in halting breaths. "Needed Luke to get the amulet and you to have time to kill the damn thing. I'm... alright..." she panted.

Luke slammed to his knees beside them both, the amulet clenched numbly in his fist.

"Emmie?" he whispered, shock making him feel cold and hot at the same time, making him feel as if he weren't even really in his body and instead watching from the outside. Dean shot him a look that made Luke flinch back and drop his eyes. The demigod was furious. And rightfully so: this was all his fault.

"I'm already...healing," she said, though she was still breathless, her skin ashen. "I'm ok. Get us out of here, Dean."

With that, Dean lifted Emmie easily with one arm beneath her knees and the other wrapped around her shoulders, careful not to touch her back. Luke forced himself to look and saw that she was right, the wounds were already slowly knitting themselves back together, but it didn't ease the ache in his chest.

"Pup!" he shouted, and Luke blinked, realizing what Dean needed him to do. He reached out and grasped Dean's shoulder, and a second later, the darkness swallowed them.

CHAPTER
SIXTEEN

They landed in the oversized downstairs hallway of their safe house, and Luke immediately dropped his hand from Dean's arm, stepping away.

"Put me down, Dean. I'm fine," Emmie insisted when it looked as if he didn't plan to let her go. Ever.

Dean lifted one blonde brow but did as she asked, his lips pressed into a hard line. She swayed slightly, but gave them both murderous glares when they moved forward to steady her. They halted and she held up a finger.

"I would like to remind you, ever so gently," she said, eyes sparkling bright lavender, her runes glowing brightly, "that I am older than both of you, older than this entire fucking universe, and would never be brought down by some ridiculous little demon." She scoffed and pretended to fluff her dust-covered hair. "It hurt like hell, but I'm already healed. See." She turned to show her back and though her shirt was shredded, the skin beneath had already knitted back together, faint pink lines where the bloody gashes had been minutes ago.

Dean's shoulder relaxed a fraction, but his eyes were burning with barely contained rage, churning like liquid gold.

"I'm going to shower," Emmie said, "I feel disgusting."

"Do you need—"

"Lucas and I are going to have a chat," Dean cut in, his voice cold and snapping like a whip.

Emmie arched a silvery brow, but nodded and turned to head upstairs. Lucas clenched his jaw when his gaze dipped to her shredded shirt again, the dried blood covering her back. The sight made his chest ache. He hadn't meant for her to get hurt. He didn't think that she'd come after him, he'd meant to do it alone.

Dean grabbed Luke by the back of the shirt and hauled him down the hallway.

"Hey," Luke protested, stumbling the first few steps from the force of Dean's grip, but he didn't seem to even hear Luke, seemed to be beyond hearing. Fire was crawling up his arms and Luke eyed the flames warily. Dean was shaking in his effort to keep control. They stopped in front of the door at the end of the hallway, and Dean finally released Luke's shirt, clenching his hands into fists at his sides.

"In here," Dean grated, shouldering the door open. Luke rolled his eyes but followed Dean inside, closing the door behind him. The room was dimly lit, a low fire burning in the hearth, but Luke could see perfectly fine. Another bedroom, just like the one he'd been using at the other end of the hallway.

"Look, Dean, I—" The rest of his words died in his throat as Dean whirled on him, slamming him back against the closed door with so much force that the wood groaned, a crack splintering through the middle like a fissure.

Dean bared his teeth as he snarled in Luke's face, "How dare you!"

"What the—" Luke said as he batted Dean's hand off of his chest. Dean let him, only to return it to his throat instead, pinning Luke hard against the door. Dean wasn't choking him—yet—but applying enough pressure that it was a bit hard for Luke to breathe, sending the clear message that he could snap Luke's neck like a twig if he wanted. Luke's nostrils flared, but he didn't try to fight back.

"Do you realize how stupid that was?" Dean seethed.

"We got the amulet, didn't we?" Lucas bit out defensively. He was well aware of how stupid it had been, but he didn't want to acknowledge it out loud.

"It almost killed her!" Dean roared.

"But it didn't!" Luke spit back. His temper was rising in response to Dean's. His claws shot long and sharp, instincts flaring in response to the threat even as other ones recoiled from the idea of hurting Dean.

"Let go of me," Luke said in a low growl. Dean glanced down and saw the claws, tilted his head as Luke's body began to shake subtly, the muscles growing bigger, ready to shift. Dean smiled a menacing smile, one that Luke didn't like being on the receiving end of. It clearly said *aw, how adorable. I'd like to see you fucking try.*

"Listen here, pup. I have loved that woman for centuries upon centuries, and I will *not* allow any harm to come to her. Do you understand me?"

"You think I don't care about her too? She's my fucking *mate!*"

Luke blinked, surprised that he'd finally said the words out loud. Well, screamed them really. He recovered himself and continued, his blood and adrenaline pumping.

"Her being hurt is unacceptable to me too." Dean tightened his grip on Luke's throat ever so slightly, and Luke's nostrils flared in irritation. "She wasn't supposed to follow me! I was putting *myself* in danger, not her!"

"And you think I'll allow that either?!" Dean roared again, and there was something in the words, something that sent a jolt through Luke's entire body.

"Wh...what?" Luke stammered. Was Dean saying...No. He couldn't be. It was wishful thinking. Dean shook his head, as if he were exasperated, or maybe even in defeat.

"Gods, you really are a stupid fucking pup, aren't you?" he said, softer. The anger leaked out of Dean, leaving fear of all things in its place. Fear and...something else. Something dangerous. Something that made Luke's heart thud loudly in his hears.

The aggression-filled tension around them shifted into something else entirely, though just as strong. Dean's grip eased, but his hand remained caging Luke's throat. His eyes had shifted to gold in his rage, and now his pupils began to expand, the black standing out starkly against the burning gold.

Before Luke even knew what was happening, his hand shot out, gripping the front of Dean's shirt and pulling him forward. Dean's eyes widened just before Luke's lips crashed against his. He froze for the briefest moment before returning the kiss with an intensity unlike anything Luke had ever experienced.

Dean shifted his grip from Luke's throat to the nape of his neck, pulling him harder against his lips. They were firm and soft and scorching, moving in a desperate frenzy that sent fire through Luke's every vein.

It was too much.

It wasn't nearly fucking enough.

But Luke had no idea what he was doing and his hands shook slightly as they tightened on Dean's shirt.

Dean whispered raggedly against his mouth, "If you don't want this, pup, tell me to stop." *Never*, Luke thought savagely. *Never fucking stop.*

He couldn't form words, so in response, Luke's hand slid downward, grasping Dean's hip and yanking him forward, pressing their bodies firmly together. Luke made a strange groaning sound and Dean hissed in a sharp breath through his teeth as their cocks met. It was a delicious agony and he needed more, more, more. He shifted his hips forward, grinding his shaft harder against Dean's and digging his fingers in so tightly he was probably leaving bruises on Dean's hip.

Or he would if the person in front of him wasn't a fucking *demigod*.

The realization made Luke feel even more completely out of his depth, but he couldn't make himself stop. This was...right. Everything in him was telling him that it was. Dean was fucking *his*, just as Emmie was. The two of them. They completed Luke in every possible way, had been destined to be his by the hand of fate. It didn't make any sense and Luke had never heard of any shifter, any supernatural creature being given two mates before, but he couldn't worry about it anymore. He knew it was true down to the very core of his being, in the deepest depths of his soul. So what if it had never happened before? He was pretty sure that a half-goddess, half-phoenix had never single-handedly defeated one of the most powerful gods in existence before Skylar had done it. So, there was a first time for everything.

"I...I don't know...what I'm doing," Luke admitted between panting breaths as Dean kissed and bit across his jaw and down his neck. Gods Luke could barely think when Dean was doing that, let alone form complete sentences. At least not any coherent ones. It took him a few extra seconds before he could bite out, "You have to... have to tell me if..."

"Keep doing what you're doing. *Don't fucking stop* doing what you're doing," Dean rasped in answer, his voice low and rough. He took Luke's mouth again and Luke dug his hand through Dean's hair, pulling at the strands. Their hips continued to move, thrusting and grinding. The friction was almost unbearable but gods was it good. Luke was dying to know what it might feel like skin on skin, nothing between them. He shot harder at the thought and couldn't stop himself from reaching down to rub his palm over Dean's shaft. It was hard as steel and seemed to be nearly bursting through his pants.

Gods, he's fucking huge.

Luke was no slouch in the size department but he thought that Dean had him beat by a good inch or two. *Holy fuck.* The thought was both intimidating and so arousing that he somehow grew even harder, his cock throbbing for release.

"Gods, Lucas," Dean rasped. The sound of his name on Dean's lips sent him into a frenzy. Already instincts were demanding... things. Things he had no idea how to approach or deal with right now, but for the moment, all he knew was that he had to get his hands on Dean or he might die. He tore at the fly of Dean's pants and shoved them down just far enough. Luke reached down, holding his breath, his heart thundering.

"Fucking hells!" Dean yelled, bucking his hips into Luke's seeking hand. Luke wrapped his fingers around Dean's cock, marveling at how hot and soft his skin was. He stroked slowly despite the ferocity of their kisses, the intensity roiling through them. Dean shuddered, his dick pulsing against Luke's palm. He stroked again. Down and slowly back up, fascinated with the feel of it. Luke swiped his thumb across the slit, spreading the bead of moisture that had already sprung up there.

"Gods, I could come already," Dean croaked. Luke stroked harder, emboldened by Dean's reactions. He trailed kisses across Dean's jaw and down his throat, and Dean braced his hands on the door on either side of Luke's head, surrendering control and letting Luke do whatever he wanted.

And fuck, he *wanted*. He wanted things he'd only thought of in passing before. Things he'd been dreaming about for weeks. Things he never knew he wanted until this moment. Too many fucking things, all slamming into him at once.

He licked and bit lightly at the spot where Dean's shoulder met his neck, the need to sink his fangs into that tender flesh and claim Dean as his own thundering through Luke's veins. No, this was too much, too new, too confusing, too intense. He couldn't...could he? *Fuck*. He needed to slow his thoughts and figure this out, to stop and talk to Dean, but when Dean groaned and lolled his head back in pure bliss as Lucas continued to stroke, there was no fucking way he could stop. Seeing a demigod so utterly lost for him was...heady.

And sexy. Definitely fucking sexy.

Luke growled low and gently raked his claws across Dean's lower back as he pulled him closer, not enough to break the skin, but enough to make Dean gasp and shudder. Luke gripped his cock harder, and stroked faster. A deep, shuddering moan rocked through Dean's chest and Luke heard the wood splinter behind him just before shards of wood pelted the side of his neck and shoulders, but he barely noticed. He would be all too happy to destroy this entire fucking room.

"Need to...touch you...too..." Dean panted.

"When I'm done with you," Luke all but snarled against his throat, surprising himself. This was *his* time. His time to enjoy, to explore, to relish in the magnificent male before him. He wanted Dean to touch him more than just about anything, but he didn't want any distractions right now. He wanted to enjoy and remember every single moment, savor it as he crossed into this new life, this new world he'd only dreamed of before.

"I want to make you come," Luke rasped as he nipped at Dean's ear lobe. Another violent shudder ran through the demigod's entire body.

"Do it then, pup," Dean said, a smile in his voice along with a bit of challenge. He tangled his fingers in Luke's hair and brought Luke's lips to his once more. He thrust his hips forward, pressing his cock harder into Luke's palm. Luke smiled against Dean's lips and shoved him forward, never loosening his grip. The two of them stumbled backwards until Dean's back slammed up against an armoire across the room with a loud thud. Something within tumbled and crashed against the doors, but neither one of them gave a shit.

The kiss was pure fire, a clash of teeth and tongues and heat. Luke stroked faster, rocking his own hips in time, needing to feel the friction as well. He spread the precum over the head and down the shaft, making his fist slide quicker.

"Oh *gods*," Dean grated, teeth clenching.

"Fuck, you feel good," Luke rasped, the words coming out like a growl.

"I'm...fuck, I'm going to come, Luke. Lift your shirt." Luke didn't know why he was doing it exactly but he didn't hesitate. He lifted the hem of his shirt and as he felt the slick head of Dean's cock pressing against his bare stomach, he understood.

And fuck, he wanted it.

"Fuckkkk," Dean gritted. He dug his fingers into the back of Luke's neck, leaning his forehead against Luke's. Luke pumped harder, faster, pressing the head of Dean's cock against his abs. Flames licked over Dean's skin, up his arms. "Going to...come!!" Dean threw his head back and roared as hot lashes of cum scalded Luke's bare stomach. Luke couldn't stop himself from glancing down, watching Dean erupt against him. It was one of the most erotic things he'd ever seen.

When Dean was finally spent, they were both breathing hard, chests heaving. Luke had no idea what to do now and stood, stunned, unbelieving that that had just happened. Dean gently eased out of Luke's grip and pulled Luke's shirt up over his head. Luke let him, raising his arms obediently. Dean used the shirt to wipe the mess from Luke's stomach, and Luke watched him as he concentrated on his task. His hair was a mess and clinging to his temples with sweat. He had dirt streaked over one sharp cheekbone and, even disheveled and dirty and bloody, he was so handsome it was nearly painful to look at him, like staring into the sun.

When Dean was done cleaning, he met Luke's gaze. They were both still breathing hard and though Dean had just come—pretty fucking hard, from the looks of it—the tension between them hadn't eased. In fact, it was even thicker than before, both of them far from done and Luke's erection pulsing so hard it was painful.

Dean reached out and cupped the back of Luke's neck, holding his gaze.

"What do you need, Lucas?" he asked, surprisingly gentle though he was clearly struggling to keep his voice even.

"I—" Luke cut himself off and swallowed hard. He couldn't say what he needed, what he wanted so desperately he could barely breathe. His cheeks heated slightly and he shifted his gaze downward. Dean dug his fingers harder into Luke's neck.

"None of that, pup. Eyes here." Luke obeyed immediately, surprised by the swift wave of fire the words sent through his stomach. "What. Do. You. Need?" There was a knowing look in Dean's eyes, but Luke knew that Dean was going to make him say it. Partly because he was a jackass, and partly because he was so far from one that it made Luke's chest twist. Dean needed Luke to say the words, to be the one to give the permission, to be the one to lead this wherever he wanted it to go.

Dean was giving Luke the reins, complete control. Luke took a deep, settling breath.

"I need...I need to claim you," Luke rushed out in a rough whisper, but he didn't avert his eyes. This was Dean. One of his best friends, a brother in blood and battle...his mate. There was nothing Luke should feel the need to hide from him, nothing he should feel ashamed of when it came to the two of them. So he let out a long breath and put it all out there. If Dean didn't feel the same, so be it, but Luke needed him to know, was tired of being afraid of the truth. "You're mine, Dean. You're mine as much as Emmie is. Both of you."

Dean's lips curled into a slow, cocky smile.

"Say that middle bit again. The part about me. I love hearing about myself, in case you've forgotten."

Luke smiled back, shaking his head in amusement at the arrogant prick in front of him. The arrogant prick that he fucking loved in a way he never thought possible. He loved Emmie with his whole heart, and yet, he loved Dean just as much, each love similar but so different too. All encompassing, yet neither could possibly lessen the other. It was complicated and surreal and confusing and amazing.

"Come on," Dean drawled, tossing his head back to shift golden strands of hair out of his eyes. "It rhymes with 'smore bine' or 'blore tine.'" Luke gave the former cat an *eat shit* look, but couldn't stop his grin. Dean acting like, well, himself, actually helped calm Luke's heart, to center him again and settle the worst of the nerves. It helped him slip back into their easy, familiar rhythms, ones that made him relax despite the incredibly tense and somewhat insane situation they were in.

Dean arched a brow in flirtatious challenge that simultaneously made Luke hard as a fucking rock and want to punch the demigod in the jaw—playfully of course. Mostly.

Alright, asshole, you asked for it. Shifters were known for being arrogant and cocky too, especially the wolves. Luke could play this game better than just about anyone. *Time to let a little bit of the wolf out*, Luke thought with a sly grin. He slowly licked his bottom lip, noting how Dean's eyes clocked the movement and enjoying the jolt of confidence it sent through his system. Oh yes, he could definitely play.

"Say. It," Dean said again, half teasing, half pleading, and Luke realized he didn't just want to hear it, he *needed* to. Luke wondered how long Dean had been hiding his feelings for him, how long he'd loved him back.

"You are *mine*," Luke said in a low, husky voice. A small shudder of pleasure rippled through Dean's entire body, his eyes sliding closed in pure contented bliss. Luke loved the look on him, but he had to disturb it. He reached out and ripped Dean's shirt apart, the shreds of fabric falling to the floor around them like confetti. Dean's eyes flew open, meeting Luke's and burning like liquid gold.

"I liked that shirt," Dean protested with a laugh as Luke's lips crashed to his again. This time, Luke was the aggressor, his tongue dominating Dean's, demanding more, and Dean let him do it. Despite being a demigod, he was letting Luke take control, be the alpha, knowing exactly what Luke needed. Lukewalked them backwards, his hands roaming over Dean's chest, the skin hot and so soft it felt like silk. Dean hooked a finger through Luke's belt loop, tugging him forward and keeping him close. When the back of Dean's thighs hit the bed, Luke pulled back just enough to speak, his lips moving against Dean's.

"You are mine," he repeated before biting on Dean's lower lip, making the demigod inhale sharply in pleasure.

"And I claim what is mine."

CHAPTER
SEVENTEEN

Dean's bones melted at Luke's words, a shudder running through him leaving a light trail of fire in its wake. He could tell that a part of Luke was still nervous about all of this—Dean knew that he'd never been with a man. Thought about it maybe, but had never done more than flirt, while Dean had been with men, women, gods, mortals, sirens, even a few demons here and there—but the cocky alpha wolf shifter was holding the nerves back for now and Dean couldn't deny that it was sexy as fuck.

"Not yet," Dean nearly growled before slanting his mouth over Luke's again. He'd let Luke do what he needed to do later, to claim him in any and every way Luke needed or wanted, but not yet. Dean hadn't had his turn yet.

He yanked Luke's pants open with such force that a button flew across the room, pinging off of something metal. Before Luke could even say a word, his cock was in Dean's hand. Luke jolted at the contact, groaning and gasping.

"So fucking hard," Dean rasped and Luke's breath hitched. Dean stroked him from base to tip, long and slow, and Luke bit his lip and ran a hand through his hair. Luke's skin was hot, hotter than most beings, but shifters usually were.

"Fuck," Luke whispered, voice ragged, "that feels good." His eyes slid shut and he was somehow tense and languid all at once. Dean grinned and slid to his knees. Luke eyes snapped open and when he glanced down, his lips parted in shock. His eyes had darkened and behind them warred two things: incredulity and desire. Dean began to lean forward, but Luke's hand shot out and gripped his shoulder, halting him.

Dean exhaled and winged an annoyed brow up at Luke.

"No, you shouldn't...you're a *demigod* for fuck's sake..."

"And this demigod is choosing to kneel before you, Lucas," he said, holding Luke's gaze. They stayed that way for an endless moment, everything Dean was saying without words slowly settling over Luke. *You are worthy. You are more than worthy. You are mine.*

Finally, Luke swallowed hard and gave a tiny nod of acceptance. Dean grinned and shoved Luke's pants down his thighs, his cock springing completely free. Long. Hard. Straining forward, the crown already slick. *Fuck me.*

Dean glanced up and said, "If you want me to stop, now's the time to say the word, pup." He gave Luke one last chance to change his mind, to decide it was all too much. Dean's control was fraying and he wanted Luke so fucking badly...

In answer Luke wrapped one of his hands over Dean's where is gripped Luke's cock. He eased the other hand to the back of Dean's head, shaking slightly. Dean's brows arched up and a grin curled his lips as Luke guided Dean's head forward, positioning the head of his cock just before Dean's mouth. *Fuck, fuck, fuck, this is hot,* Dean though, heart hammering in his chest, blood literally on fire, flames dancing across his skin.

In a rough voice, Luke said, "Don't even fucking think about stopping."

Thank the fucking gods. Dean leaned in and ran his tongue over the head of Luke's cock before closing his lips around it.

"Holy fuck," Luke groaned, fingers digging into the back of Dean's head. Dean released him, only to lick down the thick shaft and slowly back up again before dipping his tongue into the slit. Luke's head lolled back and he made low, guttural growls of pleasure that made Dean's cock pulse, already hard again. He watched Luke's throat bob as he swallowed hard, his head still thrown back, his jaw clenching as he fought against the pleasure.

"Don't you want to watch, pup?" Dean whispered in a low voice.

Luke's eyes flew open and he jerked his gaze downward. Dean smirked, holding Luke's gaze as he fed Luke's cock back between his lips, twirling his tongue before sucking hard.

"Oh dear gods," Luke croaked. "Dean...*oh my gods*." His eyes were wide and almost completely black. Luke's legs shook subtly and his hips arched forward as Dean continued to lick and suck. He gripped Luke's hips and Luke tensed, probably thinking Dean wanted him to stop thrusting, but in reality, he fucking *loved* it. Dean tugged Luke's hips towards him on his next glide forward, sending Luke deeper into his throat, repeating the movement again on the next glide down Luke's cock. By the next time, Luke had gotten the message, and he thrust his hips forward on his own. Still gently, but it was fucking *glorious*.

"Ah, fuck," Luke panted. "Seeing me...fuck your mouth...Gods, it's too fucking good." Dean groaned, cock pulsing at Luke's words. Luke thrust again, a bit more forcefully while holding the back of Dean's head, claws digging into his scalp, and Dean might just come again from it. Dean dug his own nails into Luke's hips, holding his gaze as Luke fucked his mouth, over and over, but then the fucker pulled away completely.

"Hey!" Dean protested, wanting Luke to come on his tongue, but Luke hauled him up off his knees with surprising strength and slammed his lips down on Dean's. Dean's hands ran over Luke's bare chest and down his arms...Dean inhaled sharply when he realized that Luke's chest and arms were definitely *bigger* than usual, the muscles growing and bulging. He was close to the edge, his wolf-nature taking over, preparing to claim his mate.

Dean's stomach clenched in anticipation and he shoved Luke back on the bed.

DEAN FOLLOWED HIM DOWN, his body hard and flaming hot against Luke's own. Luke couldn't stop touching him, couldn't stop running his hands all over Dean's body. He heard Dean's boots hit the floor and he quickly kicked off his own. He shoved at Dean's pants and when Dean shifted to get them off, Luke ripped his own away as well. There was no shyness or apprehension now. Now there was only an animistic, burning desire that couldn't be denied much longer.

Dean settled beside him and Luke turned, reaching between them to grip Dean's cock and his own together in his hand. They both hissed in quick breaths between clenched teeth at the feeling of flesh on flesh, and then they both laughed lightly at their identical reactions. Luke still didn't know what the fuck he was doing, really, but he just let his body guide him, doing what felt right.

Dean settled his larger hand over Luke's and they both slowly stroked together.

"Fuck, Luke," Dean rasped in a low, hoarse whisper, before pressing his lips to Luke's again.

The sensations were so new, so different, so intense. The two of them stroked slowly, despite the frenzied need riding them, savoring the feel of each other. Luke's breaths began to grow quick and shallow, the pleasure so intense it was bordering on pain. Luke's instincts were screaming at him, his nails and fangs lengthening, his cock harder than it had ever been and pulsing with the need to...

Fuck. Luke's cheeks flushed as he realized he really didn't quite know how to approach this part, and he pulled away from Dean.

Reading his mind as always, Dean said, "Out with it, pup."

"I...I don't really know...I mean, I need to...but don't you need to... um, like...prepare?" Luke said, feeling like his face was on fire.

Dean grinned, chuckling lightly, and Luke pulled his hand free, throwing them both over his face.

"Fuck. Off," he said from behind his fingers. How he could be simultaneously mortified and hornier than he'd ever been in his entire fucking existence?

"Well, I'm trying, but you're being entirely inarticulate," Dean said breezily.

"I hate you," Luke said, lowering his hands to glare...but also to grip Dean's cock again because he honestly couldn't stop himself. His lips curled into a satisfied smirk when Dean's hips jerked forward and he had to clear his throat before speaking.

"One: no you don't, you love me. Two: I love you too, in case you haven't figured that out yet." Luke's heart stuttered. He'd thought it was the case but to hear it...Gods, all was fucking right with the world in this moment. Dean continued on, "Three: if I were a mortal man, with a mortal, human body, then yes, a little prep work would be necessary in that department..." His eyes burned as he leaned in and kissed Luke deeply, as if he just couldn't help it, his tongue rough and hot against Luke's.

"But I am not a mortal man and I do not have a mortal body, Lucas," he added in a sexy whisper. "My body can...adapt to things in ways a mortal body can't. Yours can as well, you know. If you were ever, uh, ya know...curious..." Now Dean's cheeks flushed ever so slightly and the sight made the knot in Luke's stomach unclench and disappear. It also made him very, *very* curious...

Luke stroked Dean's cock again, rubbing the head against his own and Luke hissed in a harsh breath.

"Noted," he nearly growled. He slammed his lips to Dean's and the kiss was all fire and passion and need. Unyielding, burning need that Luke could never have imagined. Somehow, within a few heartbeats, they'd shifted and Dean was on his hands and knees before Luke.

"Fuck," Luke whispered as the sight. Luke reached out, curiosity and lust mixing together as he ran a hand over Dean's ass, the muscles taut and flexing beneath his fingers. He slowly trailed his fingers downward and pressed a finger over Dean's hole, rubbing gently. It must be sensitive because Dean arched his back with a panting moan. *Interesting.*

"Pup," he groaned, "You're fucking killing me here."

Luke's need to claim his mate won out over his insane curiosity about every aspect of this new facet of his life, all of the possibilities, all of the places his imagination was running rampant. He shifted forward, using his knees to spread Dean's a little wider, and, without knowing what else to do, he spit into his hand, rubbing the saliva over his cock. He positioned the head at Dean's entrance and nearly shuddered in pleasure and anticipation.

"You're...sure?" he grated out through clenched teeth.

"If you don't fucking do it, Lucas, I will," Dean nearly growled.

"I'm going to hold you to that one day," Luke said quietly and Dean rasped out a low, *"fuck,"* in response.

With that, Luke gripped his cock and slowly eased his hips forward, watching in utter stunned fascination and desire as he slipped inside.

It was tight. *Fuck* was it tight. Tighter than a fist. But *fuck. Me. Running.* It was amazing. Perfect. He'd never done this before, with anyone, and the fact that he hadn't made this moment even more perfect, he thought. He liked that he was having more than one first with Dean.

Luke forced himself to go slowly. Dean claimed his body could adjust to things the way a human body couldn't, but still, Luke didn't want to test those boundaries and cause him any pain. Dean let out a low, guttural moan, his entire body going rigid.

"Alright?" Luke bit out. One hand was still wrapped around the base of his cock, feeding it inside Dean, and the other rested on Dean's hip.

"Fucking amazing. *Keep going.*"

Luke pressed forward harder, losing some of his hesitancy because of Dean's intense reactions and the tight heat surrounding his cock so thoroughly he could barely think.

"Fuck!" Luke cried out as he finally lost control and surged forward, bucking into Dean until their bodies were flush and Luke's cock was buried to the hilt.

Oh. My. Gods.

"Lucas," Dean rasped, the word somehow a plea and a prayer all at once, as if he'd been waiting his entire life to say it. Amid the most intense pleasure he'd ever experienced, lust and need nearly consuming him like an inferno, Luke's heart clenched at the sound, the final piece of the puzzle clicking into place with an almost audible *thunk*. Maybe Dean *had* been waiting his whole life to say the word,

"Fuck you feel good, Dean. Fucking amazing. Oh my Gods..." Luke pulled back and drove his hips forward again, fingers and claws digging into Dean's hips. Blood welled, but Dean didn't seem to notice or care. Again and again and again, Luke lost himself in Dean, everything else in the entire universe fading away to nothing. Nothing else existed, nothing else mattered. The amulet and this fucking realm they were still stuck in, the coming darkness that Emmie had warned them of, anything and everything outside of the two of them, here, in this moment, simply couldn't touch him.

"Gods, it feels good, Luke. Your cock filling me up so fucking full..."

Luke shuddered at the words, loving that Dean was a talker too. He thrust his hips faster, fucking Dean harder than he could have imagined being able to, watching himself sink deep into Dean's body over and over. Dean clawed at the sheets, arched his back, and rocked his hips backward in time with Luke's thrusts. Luke ran his fingers down Dean's spine, over the lines of his tattoos.

"One day, you'll tell me what these say," he panted. "But right now, I want you to tell me again how good I feel inside you, how much you like my cock filling you up."

Dean made a sound that was half groan-half moan, and entirely fucking sexy, and then acquiesced to Luke's needy demand. Dean's words were like molten lava flooding through Luke's veins. Every dirty musing, every word of praise, every unintelligible curse was somehow hotter than the last. Luke called on every last ounce of self-control he had in order to hold out, not to come yet. He'd almost come the second he slid inside, it had been so tight, so overwhelming, but he'd managed to bite back the urge, to focus his thoughts and control his body, but only barely. Now, it was almost impossible.

"Ah gods, I'm going to come, pup," Dean groaned and Luke's eyes flew wide.

"Really?" he asked, not able to stop the question. Dean seemed to be, uh, *enjoying* himself if his grunts and groans and the most artful dirty talk Luke had ever heard (and was now addicted to) were any indication, but was it really good enough for him to get off?

Dean looked over his shoulder, arching a brow, sweat trickling down his temples, his hair damp with it.

"Are you seriously asking me that?" He shifted and pulled Luke down, guiding Luke's hand around their joined bodies until his grip found Dean's cock. Luke obediently wrapped his hand around it and inhaled sharply. So fucking hard, practically pulsing, the head slick. Luke's eyes slid closed with a low groan.

"Feel that? *That's* how hard you fucking me makes me." He shifted his hips and forced his cock harder into Luke's palm, and added, "You say the word, and I'll show you just how good this feels, pup."

Luke's entire body shuddered, suddenly wanting very, very much for Dean to show him. To show him everything possible. Dean forced Luke's hand away and shouldered him back.

"No, fuck me, Lucas," he demanded.

Luke obeyed, embolded by just how much Dean seemed to be loving this, and gripped Dean's hips again. Luke pulled his hips back, his cock sliding almost completely out, before slamming them forward again, wrenching Dean's hips backward at the same time.

"FUCK," Dean groaned. "Again!"

"Gods, you take my cock so fucking well, Dean. Fuck, fuck, fuck..." Luke gnashed his teeth as he slammed into Dean over and over and over. They were both breathing hard, chests heaving and bodies slicked with sweat. Luke knew he wouldn't last much longer now, and his instincts flared. *Bite. Claim. Yours.*

"Need to..."

"Oh I know exactly what you need, Lucas," Dean said, somewhere between a growl and a purr and Luke nearly came just from the sound of his voice. Luke clenched his teeth, his fangs nearly slicing through his lower lip. Dean shifted so that he was upright on his knees, his back to Luke's chest and Luke's cock still buried deep inside him. He turned and kissed Luke hard before turning away again and tilting his head, exposing his throat.

Luke couldn't hold back any longer. He leaned down and ran his tongue down Dean's throat as he wrapped his arm around Dean's body, gripping his cock. The demigod let out a long, low groan as Luke stroked while thrusting his hips forward.

"You're mine," Luke rasped against Dean's ear, the words low and rough and so damned life-altering that Luke couldn't wrap his mind around it.

"And you're fucking mine," Dean responded, reaching back to grip the back of Luke's head and shove his mouth against Dean's neck. Luke sank his fangs into the spot where Dean's throat met his shoulder, the flesh tender and giving. His eyes flashed wide and a growl rumbled in this chest.

"*FUCK!*" Dean roared. Luke thrust his hips forward once, twice more, pumping his fist over Dean's cock in time with thrusts, and kept his fangs clamped on Dean's neck. Dean's entire body tightened and then shuddered beneath Luke as he came in a rush. Hot and wet and too fucking arousing. Flames licked up and down his arms, across his shoulders and back, but they didn't hurt Luke. In fact, they felt good against his skin.

Luke roared Dean's name as he came harder than he ever had,

pounding into Dean until he had nothing left. He collapsed hard onto Dean's back, his knees giving out and tremors rocking his entire body. Luke didn't know how the hell dean was holding them both up, but then remembered that his mate was a fucking demigod.

Luke withdrew his fangs and leaned his forehead against Dean's shoulder. They were both panting, bodies trembling and covered in sweat. Somehow, Luke managed to pull his boneless body away from Dean's and they both turned to sprawl across the bed on their backs.

After a few minutes of silence, their loud, heavy breaths the only sounds in the room, Dean laughed. Lightly at first and then louder, and soon his entire body was shaking with it.

Luke bolted upright, a surge of uncertainty and...a little embarrassment crashing through him like a tank. Had he done something wrong?

"And what, pray tell, is so fucking funny?" he asked in a clipped tone.

Dean stopped laughing for a second, meeting Luke's gaze and then cracking up again, his smile so light and easy that, despite Luke's growing urge to break the demigod's nose, his chest warmed at the sight.

"What the fuck? What are you—"

Dean's hand whipped out and wrapped around the back of Luke's neck, yanking him forward into a soul-searing, bone-melting kiss. Luke's brows furrowed, but he didn't pull away, didn't dare try to stop the kiss. After what could have been a fucking lifetime, Dean pulled away, grinning.

"Are you going to let me in on the joke?"

Dean exhaled, huffing out another little laugh.

"Fate. Fate is a funny, fickle, brilliant bitch." When Luke just looked on in confusion, Dean continued, "I've been trying to lift that curse for centuries, and it just occurred to me that if I had succeeded in any of the thousand attempts, it would have been... wrong. I needed to wait until now. I needed to wait for *you*." He sighed, utter contentment radiating from every line in his body.

"And I would do it all again, Luke. I'd wait another hundred years, a thousand."

A lump formed in Luke's throat, the gravity of what Dean was saying settling over him like a ten ton blanket.

He cleared his throat roughly and said, "I would have waited for you too." *For both of you*, he thought, Emmie's beautiful face flashing behind his eyes. Suddenly, everything from outside came rushing back in again, and he tensed, having no idea what happened now. He had two mates. Emmie and Dean loved each other. How did all of this work? Did they just...take turns? A flash of the three of them together made Luke's cock jump and his blood boil, but...could that really work? The three of them, together?

As if thinking of Emmie had summoned her, she breezed into the room, silvery hair shining like a quicksilver river over one shoulder. She wore a tank top and silk shorts that were so short, they barely covered anything at all. She didn't seem at all surprised to see the two men sprawled across the bed together, very sweaty and very, very naked.

"Emmie," they both said at the same time, and her lips curled upward.

"About damn time," she said in response. "Silly boys." She rolled her eyes and made her way to the bed. With a wave of her fingers and a flash of light, the mess they'd made of the bed was cleaned, fresh sheets and blankets suddenly below their backs, their bodies clean and sleep pants hanging low on both their hips.

"What the..."

"She's very handy, pup," Dean said with a grin.

Emmie winked and crawled onto the bed. The two of them shifted as she shooed them with her hand, making it clear they were to move to the top of the bed and make room for her.

Luke opened his mouth to speak, to voice the question, but Emmie cut him off with a quick kiss. "Later," she said. "We'll figure it out later. For now, we all need rest. We have a big day tomorrow."

She snuggled down into the blankets, putting her back against

Dean's chest and wrapping his arm around her stomach, and draping her arm over Luke's. Luke met Dean's eyes over Emmie's head and he shrugged a shoulder, as if to say *she makes the rules, I just follow orders.*

Later. They would figure it all out later. Luke decided to just go with it for now. He relaxed, letting the utter rightness of all of this settle over him and exhaustion drag him down.

"Tomorrow, we exterminate an entire cult of goblins," Emmie added quietly just before darkness claimed Luke. There was a smile in her voice, and he was reminded once again, that Emmie was as terrifying as she was beautiful.

EIGHTEEN

Emmie was ready to be done with this place. She was ready to kick ass, take names, and get the fuck home. She had things to do and evil enchantments to lift and plans to put into motion that may or may not equal the end of the world as they knew it but were absolutely necessary. Oh, and a wedding to plan!

So, it was time to finish this.

They made their way through the hidden tunnel that led back to the dungeons, Dean in front, Emmie in the middle, and Luke bringing up the rear, the two boys on full alert. Emmie was ninety-seven percent sure that everything was going to go according to plan, but it was still better to be prepared for anything, just in case. Her runes glittered faintly in the dim tunnel.

"Did you know that digging tunnels isn't very exciting?" Dean said casually.

"Huh?" Luke grunted from just behind Emmie.

"Nah, it's actually really boring. Get it. *Boring*. As in—to bore a hole."

Emmie laughed lightly and Luke sighed.

"You would think after thousands of years of life, you'd have better jokes."

"Oh come on, pup, that was a good one!"

"Hmm, gods must have a very different definition of the word *good*."

Emmie glanced back and found Luke smirking, looking somehow both more relaxed and more tense than she'd ever seen him. She knew he was having trouble wrapping his mind around the entire situation. Two mates. Two god (or god-adjacent anyway) beings as his mates. Two god-adjacent mates who were also in love with each other in addition to being in love with him.

Luke may be an immortal, a supernatural being, but he spent his life on the Mortal Plane and on the whole, mortals had trouble broadening their adorable little minds to accept things they viewed as unconventional. Emmie rolled her eyes at the thought, but kept walking. Luke would come to terms with everything in his own time. She wouldn't push and neither would Dean, but...she nearly shuddered, catching glimpses of possible futures if and when Luke chose the path she desperately hoped he did, possible futures that included the three of them, naked and writhing and—

"Emmie," Luke hissed quietly and she was fairly certain he'd called her name at least twice already.

"Hmm? What? I wasn't thinking about anything dirty, I swear." Dean barked out a laugh and Luke's lips curled up when she met his gaze, giving him a sultry look that told him exactly what direction her thoughts had been taking.

"Focus," Luke chided with a wink.

"Ok, you're right. Dirty thoughts later. Rescue mission-slash-massacre now."

Both men laughed but quieted as they neared the end of the tunnel, low light seeping in from beneath the hidden door.

"I still don't know why I couldn't just phase us into the cell, grab the bitch—sorry, the enchantress—and get the hell out of here." Dean sounded pouty, though Emmie knew he was also weirdly thankful for the curse. If it hadn't been for Sabina, for the curse and her subsequent capture that led to the curse lasting as long as it did, he might never have found Luke. *Fate is a funny, funny thing.*

"I told you, I saw us in this tunnel. There's a reason for it. Don't you trust me after all these years?"

"With my life," Dean said easily.

"Ditto," Luke agreed. "Alright then, let's go."

The three of them shouldered their way through the door—straight into a waiting horde of goblin cultists, all pointing swords and spears their direction.

"Well, shit," Luke breathed.

"Oopsie," Emmie said with a grimace.

THE LITTLE BASTARDS SHOVED LUKE, Dean, and Emmie to their knees on a dais inside a massive stone room. It was filled with rows upon rows of granite pews, each pew occupied by hundreds of robe-clad goblins. Others in armor lined the walls.

Dean tried to keep calm. Emmie would have seen if they all ended up dead in this gods-forsaken-excuse for a church, right? He trusted she had a plan, that they would get out of this somehow. The corridor in the dungeons had been too tight for them to fight back against the throng of goblin soldiers, not outnumbered as they were. So, they'd been taken, their hands bound behind their backs, and escorted—none too gently—through the compound to what Dean understood to be their sacrificial chamber. Emmie and Luke had seen it previously, but this was the first time Dean had the pleasure.

The dais beneath them was stained with brown-black splotches that could only be blood. Lots, and lots of blood. And it reeked of death and desecration.

Sabina was sitting in a high-backed, gilded chair, hands bound to the thick arms. She struggled, eyes wild. This had clearly never happened before in all the years she'd been held here. Probably not the best sign.

Luke's shoulder pressed against his.

"Any thoughts?" he muttered, eyes scanning the crowd.

"Not yet," Dean said, weighing options, coming up with plans and back up plans. He met Emmie's eyes where she was being held between two goblins a few feet away. She shook her head minutely at him, telling him not to make a move. He hated it, his entire soul rebelling at the idea of sitting here and doing nothing while she and Luke were in danger, but he trusted Emmie. Trusted her not only with his life, but Luke's.

"We hold for now," Dean said quietly. He felt Luke stiffen beside him, but saw his nod of acceptance out of the corner of his eye.

"The time has finally come!" a goblin in a crimson robe bellowed from the center of the dais, spreading his arms wide. "Valen will return this very day!"

A chorus of "blessed be her name!" rang out among the crowd, all of them thumbing their fists over their chests three times, the movements so perfectly in unison it was creepy.

"After all of our waiting, all of our sacrifices, our loyalty is being rewarded! This...creature," he said, gesturing to Emmie, "holds power unlike we have seen, power that will finally be enough to call Valen to us once more."

Luke and Dean glanced at each other. Rage rose in Dean's chest. Were these little pricks really going to try sacrifice his—*their*—woman?

"Over my dead fucking body," Luke growled, surging forward, but he was held fast by a guard and the tip of a sword was at his throat a heartbeat later.

"That comes after our goddess arrives," the guard sneered. "Your deaths will be the first gifts we bestow upon her."

"So, I'm the appetizer, and they're the main course?" Emmie protested. "I am main course material, my friends. Main course all the way." She said it casually, but her runes shimmered as she eyed the sword at Luke's throat.

The master of ceremonies or high priest or Duke of Delusional Idiots or whatever the fuck his title was, spread his arms wide again.

"Blessed Valen, we spill this blood in your exalted name, in offering of power so that you may rise again and command your faithful servants."

The crowd began to chant, "blessed be her name," over and over quietly. *Definitely fucking creepy.*

"Come back to us, oh great one!"

Sabina struggled harder against her bonds, desperate to escape. This was very, very bad. Just as Dean was about to say fuck it all and try to fight their way out, one of the goblins shoved a gleaming golden blade through Emmie's stomach. She gasped and fell to her knees. The guards released her as blood began to pour from the wound, and Dean and Luke both roared in utter rage, bucking against their captors.

"NO!" Luke roared, his body shuddering and beginning to change. Dean's power flared, flames erupting across his skin, but his blood was as cold as ice.

Emmie toppled to the ground as the goblin stabbed her a second time.

CHAPTER

NINETEEN

This was it. This was the vision she'd had all those months ago at Hades and Skylar's wedding celebration. The one of her on the ground, surrounded by blood, reaching out for Luke and Dean, her heart screaming for both of them.

She nearly laughed now. Visions were tricky bitches sometimes. This is what she had seen, but she hadn't understood the situation, hadn't had the whole picture in that small flash.

She hadn't known that it was all part of her own brilliant plan and she was giving an Oscar-worthy performance, if she said so herself.

She could see Luke's body straining, his muscles growing and his body shuddering as he began to shift.

"Emmie!" he screamed, struggling against the guards holding him. Dean's eyes were burning gold, fire dancing along his skin, but she met his gaze and winked at him. His brow furrowed but he leaned close and whispered something to Luke. Luke whipped his head towards Dean, their eyes locking, and though he seemed confused and incredulous, he gave a curt nod and forced his body to stop shifting.

Emmie cut her eyes to Sabina and gave one surreptitious nod. The enchantress' lips curled up the tiniest bit before she schooled her features. *Show time.*

Sabina screamed bloody murder and bowed her back, as if she was in agony, straining against the bonds that held her to the gilded throne. A stream of golden power surged from Sabina towards Emmie.

"Yes! Yes, Valen! Take your power from your decedent! Rise!" the psychotic little zealot yelled, and Emmie barely stopped from rolling her eyes, remembering to keep up the act. She was supposed to be in agonizing pain, her blood being sacrificed and her body being offered up as a vessel to Valen's dead ass. Granted, two blades to the gut didn't feel *great* by any means, but she would survive, no biggy.

"No!" Sabina screamed. "No, please! No!" She bucked and shrieked and clawed at the arms of the chair before the golden stream of power surged brighter before disappearing completely. Sabina's body slumped lifelessly in the throne and her head lolled to the side. *Dramatic. I like it. Oh, right, my turn.*

Emmie screamed and bowed and shuddered, black smoke and electricity swirling around her prone body. A few seconds later, the smoke disappeared and Emmie rose, her body now that of the long-dead enchantress queen. Bone-white skin, raven black hair, blood red lips. Her eyes were wholly black and she tilted her head at the cult leader in front of her, his mouth agape.

"V-Valen," he whispered, reverently, voice trembling.

"Kneel," Emmie said in an icy voice. The leader immediately dropped to his knees and bowed so low, his forehead kissed the blood-stained stones. She turned her head to the crowd. "All of you," she commanded, "kneel before me."

Like a wave, the entire congregation followed their leader, falling to their knees, many of them crying out in disgusting joy. The guards remained standing, their weapons still raised.

"All. Of. You," Emmie ground out, black power sparking along her fingertips. The guard's all cowered, quickly bowing with the rest, their weapons tossed aside.

Emmie met Dean and Luke's gazes as their bonds fell away and they both stood, confused. She winked and grinned, and then nodded to a now fully alert Sabina, striding to stand on Emmie's right side. She had vengeful fire in her eyes, gold sparking at her fingertips. She touched a finger to the amulet around her neck—the amulet Emmie had very stealthily delivered to her the night before when the boys were sleeping and filled her in on the plan—and grinned at Emmie.

She was ready for vengeance. So was Emmie.

"You have all sacrificed in my name. You have spilled blood of the innocent." Emmie let the false face fall away, shifting back into herself. "And now," she said, the change in her voice making the goblins' eyes snap upward again. "You will pay for it," Emmie finished with a wicked grin.

Sabina's power flared, flashing out and turning the guard's weapons to dust beneath their fingers as they scrambled for them. Large wooden beams fell into the slots across both of the doors with a resounding boom. The goblins cried out as they realized they were locked in with four very, *very* pissed off supernatural beings.

"Game on," Emmie said, smiling, just as the screaming began.

THINGS WERE...COMPLICATED. Gods, how many times could Luke use the word *complicated* before it lost all meaning? He must be nearing the limit.

They'd brought Sabina back, removed the enchantment that Calypso had placed on Poseidon—which was *extremely* fucked up, in Luke's humble opinion—tossed Calypso's ass out of Aqueous for good, and watched Si and Beck tie the knot.

But what they hadn't done? Talked.

They'd all sat together at the wedding, Dean's arm around

Emmie's shoulder, Luke's hand on her thigh, and Luke and Dean exchanging glances over Emmie's head throughout. Heated glances. Glances that said they were both thinking of what had happened the other night, both wanting so much more.

But now that they were back in the real world—sort of, anyway—things felt...different. Being back, reality came crashing in. How was this actually supposed to work? Luke had no fucking clue. He loved them both, needed them both, was bound to them both. And yet, could he *be* with them both? And while he was with both of them, they would be with each other? Was that a thing? They just... traded off? Alternated weekends and holidays like kids in a custody arrangement?

"What the fuck?" he grated under the shower spray. He rested his hands on the tile, bowing his head, and letting out a long, rough, exhale. He knew they needed to figure this out, and to be honest, he knew that he was the reason they'd avoided the conversation until now. Every time it looked as if Emmie or Dean were going to bring it up, Luke changed the subject or had something he needed to do elsewhere. He was being chicken shit and he knew it, but he just wasn't ready to face it if the answer turned out to be something he didn't want.

But what the fuck *did* he want?

As the water pelted down, he forced himself to think about it, to really think about what he wanted. He forced every other extraneous detail away. What people might think, whether it was strange or confusing. None of that shit mattered.

What do I want?

The future flashed behind his eyes, as if he were the one with visions instead of Emmie. The three of them, together. Forever. He was tired of holding back and of being afraid that it might not be what they wanted. They needed to have a discussion at the very least. He couldn't live without either of them, but this was all new to him. He needed to understand what everyone was thinking and feeling and wanting and expecting.

He got dressed and felt better knowing that he was finally going to have *the talk*, but as he finished tying his boots, something ripped through his chest. Instincts reared up, telling him that something was very, very wrong.

His mate was in danger.

Luke moved like a blur through the palace, somehow knowing exactly where to go. He burst into the throne room and his breath left him: Dean was lying on the floor, covered in blood.

"What the fuck happened?" he demanded, fury and fear roiling through him like liquid fire.

"Big fight. Lots of stabby stabby. I won—mostly." Dean attempted a smile but it turned into a grimace and he gasped in pain. Luke rushed forward and he and Emmie steadied Dean long enough for her to phase them to Emmie's room. They managed to get him to the bed and he collapsed heavily. Hot blood gushed from the gaping hole in his side and he gnashed his teeth. Gods where the fuck had he been? What had happened? Who had done this to him? Why wasn't he healing??

Rage felt like a caged beast in Luke's chest, the need to protect and avenge clawing inside him with jagged claws. But there was also terror.

"Need to...find Beck..." Dean grated between panting breaths. He shook himself, as if his vision was wavering and apprehension filled Luke's veins. He couldn't...die from these injuries, right? He was a demigod, surely he would be ok?

"You need to rest and heal, you stupid fuck," Lucas grated as he sat on the edge of the bed beside Dean's legs. He clenched his jaw and settled a hand on Dean's ankle, squeezing gently.

"Has anyone...ever told you...how cute you are when you're... worried, pup?" Dean huffed out between labored breaths. Lucas wanted to laugh and strangle him at the same time. Mostly, he wanted to fix him, to somehow make him ok, to erase the clear signs of pain from his face, to take that pain into himself instead.

But he couldn't. He could only sit here and watch as one of the loves of his fucking life lie suffer and maybe bleed out. Luke finally did something sensible and balled up a blanket from the end of the bed and pressed into Dean's side. He winced, but didn't force Luke's hands away.

"I thought I was cute all the time?" Lucas said with a half-smile.

"You got me there," Dean said before a coughing fit seized him, blood spewing from his mouth.

"Gods, Emmie do something!" Luke yelled, leaping to his feet, squeezing his hands into fists and fighting the tremors racking through his body. He began to pace beside the bed, feeling useless and burning with the desire to do *something*.

Finally, the coughing fit subsided and Dean collapsed back onto the pillows.

"Bloody hell, been a while since I've had proper battle wounds. Fuck, this hurts," Dean laughed before wincing.

"I'll deliver the message," Emmie said in a soft voice, gently stroking his cheek. "Rest now."

"When I wake up, we're having a bloody long chat," he said, eyeing them both determinately, his gaze lingering on Luke. He gave the demigod a quick nod, and with that, Dean's eyes slid shut and his body went limp.

"Can you fix him?" Luke demanded. "What the fuck happened?" He tried to stop pacing, but he couldn't quite manage it.

"Something that had to happen," Emmie said quietly.

Luke stopped in tracks and turned slowly to face her.

"You knew," he whispered and he couldn't hide the accusation in his voice. "Whatever the fuck happened to Dean, you *knew* it was going to, didn't you?"

"Yes," she said simply, but she flinched slightly.

"And you just let him—"

She whirled on him, runes flaring, eyes flashing with an anger he'd rarely seen on her beautiful face.

"I *have* to let things happen, Lucas," she snapped. "I cannot stop the tapestry from flowing, I cannot shield everyone in all of the worlds from pain or even death. I can only try to steer things towards the best possible outcome, and I know you can't possibly begin to understand, but sometimes I have to be cruel to be kind. I *have* to let people hurt, people that I *fucking love* and would rather die than see harmed or in pain. I have to let them claw and fight and make their own choices and fight their own battles, and I have to just sit back and fucking pray that they come out on top, that the vision of the future that I've seen where they succeed comes to pass. Do you have any idea what that could be like?!" There were unshed tears in her eyes and her body trembled. "Do you have any fucking idea how hard it is? How terrifying? How gut-wrenching!? Do you—"

Luke crossed to her in a few long strides, cutting her off by pulling her hard against his chest and wrapping his arms around her. He felt like an absolute asshole. He'd never thought of it like that, not really, but of course he should have. He should have understood the weight that was on her shoulders and the pain she had to endure daily. He palmed the back of her head as she shuddered against him, and gently stroked her hair as she cried.

"I'm sorry. I'm a dick. Of course I can't imagine...I shouldn't have blamed you."

She sniffled and pulled away. "I get it. Everyone always blames the Seer." She shrugged and gave him a half-smile. "I've done it too. I tossed my brother into a demon realm in the Underworld completely naked with nothing but a plastic spork as a weapon when he saw something of Persephone's attempted murder of Hades and didn't say anything to stop it." Luke chuckled lightly. "Of course, I under-stood later why—he saw our Skylar long before I did—but still. I wasn't happy with him at the time."

They sat on the bed and watched over Dean as Emmie filled him in on everything that had happened, all of the history with the Dark Ones. They were the evil versions of the gods that were insanely scary and powerful, pretty much invincible, and had been locked away in Pandora's Box—which was apparently a prison, not a little chest filled with chaos like the mortal tales said. She told him that the Box was failing and that soon, lots of baddies would be released before, eventually, the Dark Ones them-selves. She told him of all of the things she'd seen coming—war and destruction and death.

"Will Si be ok?"

She sighed heavily. "That's up to Beck." She checked the nonexistent watch on her wrist. "Speaking of which, it's time for me to go break the news and send her on her rescue mission."

She disappeared and Luke shifted closer to Dean. The demigod was sleeping restlessly, a sheen of sweat covering his brow and plastering his hair to his temples, but when Luke checked his wound, he sighed in relief: it was finally closing and healing. He was going to be ok. He brushed Dean's hair from his brow and even in sleep, the demigod seemed to know that he was there and sighed, leaning his head into Luke's touch.

Luke leaned down and kissed him on the temple before settling in beside him and doing the only thing he could for now: wait.

CHAPTER
TWENTY

Luke waited for what felt like a lifetime, though it was only a few days. Dean finally woke up, healed and sullen when Emmie filled him in on Si's situation. They all sat in tense silence, all of them in their own heads it seemed, while they waited for Beck to bring Si out of his unending nightmare. Emmie sat in an oversized chair in front of the fireplace, staring into the flames, her eyes going vacant every so often as she looked to the future. She appeared drawn and strained, her slender body tense, and it was killing Luke to see her that way.

Skylar brought food, though none of them really ate much, and she didn't stick around to chat. Luke knew that she not only wanted to get back to Hades to wait with him while his brother's fate hung in the balance, but she could also sense the unease in the room.

"Umm, you'll fill me in later?" she asked Luke quietly when she hugged him goodbye.

"As soon as I know what the fuck is going on," he muttered. She eyed him, telling him without words that she was there for him no matter what, and love for her bloomed in his chest. Not the same kind as he had for Emmie and Dean, he understood that now, but love all the same. She was his family and always would be. Skylar blew Dean a kiss, waved to Emmie who barely even acknowledged her, and then phased away.

Luke paced and Dean shot him an annoyed glance from the bed, where he sat running a whetstone over the blade of a sword. Luke arched a brow in challenge, daring the demigod to tell him to stop. Dean clenched his jaw but said nothing. They were all tense, for too many reasons to name, and each handling it in their own way.

Finally, Emmie gasped and the two men jerked their heads her way, eyes wide. Was that a good gasp, or a bad one? After an interminable moment, her shoulders relaxed and a slow smile slid across her face.

"She did it. He's out. He's ok."

Dean met Luke's gaze and the annoyance and hostility from before vanished, both of them grinning, relief practically radiating from both of them. Emmie unfolded herself from the chair and strolled over, looking better than she had in weeks, and sat on the foot of the bed. She patted the spot beside her with a meaningful look at Dean. He placed the sword and stone on the bedside table and moved to sit beside her, leaning back on his hands casually, a small smirk tilting his lips upward on one side. Luke stood before them, not quite sure what was happening, and Emmie looked at him expectantly.

"Ok, now that that little problem is solved—you're up, buttercup."

Luke's brow furrowed. "What?"

"Tell us what you want, Lucas," Dean said, as if he and Emmie had been planning this. "We know this situation is...odd, and might be especially confusing and hard for you to navigate, so we need you to tell us what you're thinking."

Oh. Luke swallowed hard. They were having the talk now. Gods, he'd been wanting to have it since before Dean was injured, but now that it was actually happening, he suddenly wasn't ready. He didn't know what to do or say or think. How did he do this? What did he say? His pulse started to race, his heart thundering loudly in his own ears.

As if sensing Luke's panic, Dean added gently, "We'll do whatever you want, Lucas, you just need to tell us what that is."

He sounded completely earnest, and Luke knew that Dean and Emmie really would do whatever he wanted. It was his decision. Luke looked between them. His mates. He thought about the terror he'd felt when he knew that Dean had been hurt, the feeling of loss whenever Emmie went to a different Plane, even for a short time. They were a part of him and would be forever. He couldn't survive without either of them.

So, what did he want?

He took a deep breath and released it slowly.

"I want—I *need*—you both."

Dean nodded. "Thank you, Captain Obvious." Luke narrowed his eyes and Dean's lips quirked up. "We know you want us both, dummy. We're each one of your mates, of course you want us. And we both love you. And we love each other," he said, glancing at Emmie.

"Okay..." Luke said slowly, not quite understanding.

Dean held his gaze, his gray eyes sparkling but serious.

"So, the question isn't if you want us, pup. It's do you want *each* of us, or *both* of us?"

Luke blinked in confusion for a second. Wasn't that the same thing?...But oh. No it wasn't. Now he understood what Dean was asking. If Luke wanted to keep things separate, to be with each of them, separately, with the two of them together as well, they were ok with that.

But they were offering more than that. They were offering what he desperately wanted. He swallowed hard and took a deep, steadying breath before he answered.

"I want *both* of you. I want the three of us, together. Not me and Emmie, and me and Dean, and you two, but all of us, like it has been ever since we started looking for a way to lift the curse. The way it's supposed to be."

Emmie's eyes fluttered closed and she sighed, her lips curling upward. Was she seeing the future—*their* future? The three of them together?

"I don't know how this works," Luke said honestly, his pulse racing as thoughts sped through his mind, images of the three of them, their life together, their bedroom...He cleared his throat quietly. "I don't know what we tell people, and I don't know the mechanics or the rules, but—"

"Easy, pup," Dean said, easing off of the bed, pure heat in his gaze. "We'll take it one step at a time. There are no rules other than everyone is always honest about what they're feeling, what they want and don't want, what they need."

"Actually," Emmie pipped up, rising to her knees on the bed. "I do have a rule. You both have to swear to always give me the crispies at the bottom of the fry container. *Always*," she said sternly, eyes darkening when the two of them turned to look at her, trying to figure out if she was joking. "It is the most important rule and the only way this relationship works. I've seen it."

Luke huffed out a laugh. "Emmie, you wouldn't be lying about having visions simply to steal the best fries, would you?"

"Bloody hells, I'm rethinking this entire relationship at this point if you love the crispies. Heathens. Both of you."

"Fuck off," Luke said before gripping the front of Dean's shirt and tugging him forward. He pressed his lips to Dean's, and Dean smiled against Luke's mouth for a moment before returning the kiss, slowly at first, but there was a barely contained fire beneath the calm. Luke's entire body tensed in anticipation, having no fucking clue what would happen next, but ready to experience it all with the two people he loved more than life itself, the two people he would do anything and everything for. He knew there was a war coming, a possible world-ending war, but they would face it together.

Luke yanked up on Dean's shirt and it was gone in seconds, bare skin now beneath Luke's fingers. Dean grabbed Luke by the nape, holding him tight as he deepened the kiss, slanting his lips and thrusting his tongue against Luke's. Luke groaned and the fire burned hotter and hotter. He knew it would be out of control soon enough. Luke's shirt joined Dean's on the floor and he bit at Dean's lip as the demigod's hands roamed over his chest and stomach, his muscles clenching in response.

Luke walked them towards the bed, pulling away when they reached the edge and turning to kiss Emmie who had been watching them raptly, sitting up on her knees. Luke wanted them both so badly he could barely breathe. Emmie sucked on Luke's bottom lip, and Luke moaned quietly, tunneling a hand into her long, silver hair. Dean crawled on the bed, settling on his knees behind her, and leaning down to kiss her neck. Luke deepend the kiss, thrusting his tongue against Emmie's as she reached out and palmed Luke's cock, hard and straining against his jeans. He groaned against her lips and felt Dean's fingers run over his hand in Emmie's hair before trailing down his arm.

Dean rasped, "Mmm, looks like our boy is hard as steel already, Em." Luke's bones melted at the words, every inch of him on fire.

Luke reached down, skating his fingers under the hem of Emmie's short dress and yanked the fabric of her panties aside. He ran his hand lightly along her lips, teasing for a second before pressing a finger deep inside. She inhaled sharply and moaned, spreading her knees farther apart to give him better access.

"And our girl is wet," Luke said, meeting Dean's gaze as he continued to lick and kiss Emmie's neck. Her head lolled to the side, her lips parted, panting quietly. Dean's eyes blazed, desire burning there like liquid gold. Luke continued to pump his finger, removing it momentarily to spread moisture up to her clit and massage there ever so lightly.

"Fuck," Emmie rasped, arching her hips forward. Dean snaked one hand around her, cupping and kneading her breast. Her nipples immediately pebbled against the thin material of her dress and

Luke's mouth watered. Dean met Luke's eyes and they somehow communicated without words, knowing exactly what each other was thinking.

Luke pulled his hand away and pulled the hem of Emmie's dress upward. Dean kissed her neck once more before putting his hands over Luke's, and easing the dress the rest of the way up. Emmie raised her arms and Dean pulled it over her head, tossing it aside.

Dean moved from behind Emmie, helping to ease her upward on the bed, Luke following their path, crawling on his knees. Emmie settled on the pillow and Dean kissed Emmie's mouth once before trailing his lips along her jaw and down her throat, eventually moving to her breast. He swirled his tongue around Emmie's nipple and Luke's cock pulsed. He rocked his hips into the bed as he watched Dean take Emmie's nipple between his lips, sucking hard. Her back arched and she moaned in pleasure, digging one hand into Dean's golden hair.

Luke kissed the inside of Emmie's thigh, slowly moving upward.

"Have a taste, pup," Dean rasped, meeting Luke's gaze as he flicked his tongue over Emmie's nipple again. Luke didn't hesitate, giving Emmie a long, slow lap of his tongue. A low rumble thundered through his chest at the taste of her, of the feeling of his tongue on her hot, slick skin. Her hips bucked upward as she made a sound that was somewhere between a scream and a gasp.

"Oh my gods." Emmie's body trembled with pleasure. Luke gazed up Emmie's body, and seeing Dean's head bent over her breast, his tongue flicking out before sucking her nipple hard as Luke ran his tongue between her lips...Well, it was the most erotic, arousing thing he'd ever seen or experienced, could ever have imagined. Dean met his gaze and the gold seemed to churn like liquid. He released Emmie's breast and reached down to run his fingers through Luke's hair before cupping the back of his head.

"Fuck, pup. I could watch you do that all fucking day." Luke rocked his hips into the bed again and reached up with one hand, brushing it over Dean's cock. Dean inhaled sharply and shifted his body, moving his hips, and thrusting his cock against Luke's palm, begging.

Luke didn't know how much of this he could take. It was all so new, so intense. The taste of Emmie on his tongue, the feel of Dean in his hand. But he needed more.

As if reading his mind, Emmie panted, "Pants. Off. Now." She didn't wait for either of them to obey, just flicked her fingers and suddenly there wasn't a shred of clothing to be seen on any of them.

Emmie and Luke both reached for Dean at the same time, and they all laughed lightly. So, this might take some practice. Emmie gripped Dean's shaft and stroked, while Luke cupped Dean's sac.

"Oh fuck!" he gasped, his body going rigid and his hips bucking. He kissed Emmie hard, and dug his fingers into the back of Luke's head, urging his mouth back to Emmie's pussy. "Don't you dare stop licking, pup," he grated.

"Wouldn't dream of it," Luke responded, leaning back in to twirl his tongue around Emmie's clit before clamping his lips around the tight bud. She groaned into Dean's mouth as Luke moved his hand to stroke Dean's shaft with Emmie.

"*Fucking hells.*"

"I'm going to...come...don't stop..." Emmie panted. Luke growled and kept up his work, moving his tongue over her clit and then pressing it deep inside her.

"Do it, Lucas. I want to see you make her come on your fucking tongue." Dean pulled away from Emmie, kneading one of her breasts while his gaze locked on Luke's. Luke held it as he licked, knowing she was close. "Fuck," Dean rasped. "Fuck this is hot, I could come just watching."

The thought made Luke's cock impossibly harder and his eyes finally slid shut as he licked with abandon. Emmie ground his pussy against his mouth, begging and whimpering until she finally came in a rush, riding his tongue.

"Fuck!" she cried out as he kept lapping his tongue, wanting to taste every last drop. The tremors finally subsided and suddenly

Luke was yanked upward by impossibly strong hands, Dean's lips slamming to his, his tongue thrusting hard against Luke's.

"Want to taste her on you," he panted between kisses, his nails digging into the back of Luke's neck.

They were both kneeling on the bed, bodies so close, and as they kissed, Emmie's hands were suddenly there, gripping them both, together. Luke made a guttural, animalistic sound at the feel of Dean's hot skin against his, Emmie's hand rubbing and stroking.

"Need you," Emmie croaked, sounding desperate.

"Which one?" Dean and Luke both said against each other lips and they both laughed.

"Both," Emmie said, a smile in her voice. "To start, I want my mouth on you," she said, pulling Luke's face away from Dean's to kiss him deep and slow, "and I want you so deep inside me that I won't be able to walk tomorrow," she said, moving to kiss Dean the same way. "And then," she said holding both of their gazes as she stroked their cocks once, twice more, "I want to *watch*. And then, I had this vision of both of you looking at me—"

"If you don't stop listing *and thens* I'm going to come just thinking about them," Luke ground out roughly, entirely truthful. All of the images flashing through his mind, the different possibilities... it sent shudders of desire through Luke's body, so hard he could barely keep upright.

"Our wish is your command, love," Dean said. "You alright with this plan, pup?"

"Fuck yes," Luke growled. Emmie grinned and maneuvered between the two of them, on hands and knees, immediately taking Luke deep in her mouth. He almost yelped in surprise, but the sound quickly transformed into a low moan.

"Gods, I didn't think I'd ever see anything sexier than your face buried in her pussy, pup, but her sucking your cock..." Dean shook his head and swiped a hand over his mouth. Emmie reached back with one hand and gripped Dean's thigh, not-so-subtly reminding him that he had a job to do as well.

Luke's eyes widened and he gently ran his hands over Emmie's back. Dean kneed Emmie's thighs apart, rubbing a hand over her pert ass. He stroked his cock as he did it, long and hard and straining, and Luke actually licked his fucking lips. Dean met his gaze and smiled a cocky, sinful smile that made Luke's stomach clench.

Reading his mind, Dean said quietly, "Can't wait for that fucking day, Lucas. I can't wait to fuck your mouth."

Luke swallowed hard, biting his lip, and arched his hips forward into Emmie's hot, greedy mouth. She moaned and wiggled her ass in the air towards Dean. He chuckled, low and rough, and ran his palm over her ass again. He shifted lower and quickly thrust two fingers inside her, pumping as he stroked himself.

"So fucking wet, love." She whimpered around Luke's cock, and Dean removed his fingers, positioning the head of his cock in their place. Luke watched raptly as he moved forward, his cock easing into Emmie's tight pussy. She groaned loudly, releasing Luke's cock for a moment to glance over her shoulder at Dean.

It was...gods, it was so fucking hot. Luke was entranced by the sight. Dean finally buried himself in her as far as he could and shuddered for a moment, the muscles in his stomach clenching in a way that made Luke want to run his tongue over them. He reached his fingers toward Luke over Emmie's back.

Without a word, Luke sucked them into his mouth, tasting Emmie on them, his eyes rolling back for a moment. He sucked hard and Dean groaned.

"Gods..." Emmie whispered before drawing Luke's shaft back between her lips, sucking him deep into her throat as Dean pulled back and thrust again from behind her. Luke released Dean's fingers and Dean ran his hand down Luke's chest, resting it there for long moment before shifting it to Emmie's hips.

"Hold on, love," he rasped before he began to thrust in earnest, the force of it shoving Luke's cock deep into Emmie's throat over and over.

"Oh fuck," Luke rasped. "Oh fuck, fuck, fuck."

"Not yet, pup. Not fucking yet," Dean demanded, and it was an order, a command from a demigod warrior who led armies. Something stood at attention inside Luke at that, something he didn't know existed. He...liked it. He was used to giving orders, not taking them for the most part, but when Dean gave them...Well, he could get used to it.

Luke forced himself to hold out, even as he watched Dean pound into Emmie, watched his cock shove inside her over and over, felt her tongue rolling over the head of his cock before she sucked hard.

"Fuck, I want..."

"Me too," Dean said, knowing exactly what Luke was thinking. Emmie seemed to know too, because she pulled back at the same time that Dean pulled out of her. She gave Luke's cock one last lick before pressing up to her knees. She cupped Luke's face lovingly before trailing her hand downward, resting her palm over his heart. She smiled as it thudded against her hand, and Dean leaned down to press a soft kiss on her shoulder.

"Ready, love?"

"Ohhhh yes," she said, eyes blazing with desire. Luke wasn't completely sure what was about to happen, but he trusted Dean and Emmie and his instincts to guide him. Dean shifted behind Emmie and ran his hands along her ass. Luke could see the muscles in Dean's arm straining as he stroked his cock while he—*oh fuck.* Emmie's eyes rolled back as Dean fingered her ass, readying her for him.

"Gods," said, the anticipation killing him.

Emmie moaned loudly a moment later as Dean slid inside. Luke reached out and palmed Emmie's breasts, kneading and her hands covered his, begging for more.

"Fuckkkk," Dean rasped, gritting his teeth. "So. Fucking. Tight."

Dean pumped into Emmie once, twice, before lifting her, resting the backs of her thighs over his elbows so her weight was no longer on the bed at all and she was completely spread open before Luke. He swallowed hard. Half nervous, half more turned on than he'd ever been in his entire existence.

"Go on, pup," Dean said with a sexy grin. "She's ready. We both are."

"Please," Emmie whisper-moaned. She reached out and rested her hands on Luke's shoulders and Luke gripped his own cock, shifting his body closer to hers so that there was hardly any space between the three of them. The way it was supposed to be.

Luke met Dean's gaze and the demigod leaned forward, kissing Luke fiercely, tongue sure and demanding. Luke pulled away and kissed Emmie as he gripped his shaft, positioning himself in the right spot. He held his breath as he arched his hips, sliding inside her wet heat and *OH. MY. FUCKING. GODS.*

Luke made a sound that was more animal than human, Emmie moaned "oh Gods," and dean hissed "holy fuck" all at the same time.

Luke could feel Dean's cock inside Emmie, the pressure it put on his own, and he thought he might explode from the pleasure of it. Their sacs touched, their thighs, and Luke tunneled one hand into Dean's hair and settled the other on Emmie's waist. He wanted no part of them not touching, wanted the three of them closer than any three beings had ever been.

"Move," Dean instructed gruffly, and Luke did as he was told. Both of them began to shift their hips, moving in perfect synchronicity as they fucked Emmie.

It was ecstasy. It was torture. It was something Luke never wanted to stop.

Normally, Luke was a talker, but he couldn't form a single fucking word as he pounded inside Emmie, as he met her eyes and then Dean's, as he could feel them both in ways he had never thought possible.

"Don't stop...harder...more..." Emmie begged, and the boys both obeyed, giving her everything she wanted. What felt like hours later, she shattered with a scream, her body squeezing both of them in pulses so tight that it nearly pushed Luke over the edge too.

"Fuck, I'm coming too," Luke ground out, thrusting and not even trying to stop himself this time.

"Ditto," Dean panted, and Luke could feel Dean's cock thrusting against his own through Emmie's body. It was all too fucking much but would never, ever be enough either. He could live for a thousand years, a million, and he would never get enough of this. He would never sate this desperate, fiery thirst for his mates.

Emmie reached one hand behind her to tunnel in Dean's hair and reached out to do the same to Luke, holding both of them as they came hard, together.

"Ah gods, can feel...both of you...scorching...fuckkkk," Emmie moaned as she came again, runes flaring so brightly they made Luke's eyes water.

They stayed like that, locked together in as many ways as possible, while their chests heaved and their bodies shuddered in the aftermath of what, for Luke anyway, had been the most mind-blowing, life-altering sex of his life. Not just sex, but complete and utter connection. The feeling of being with both of his mates, of the three of them together, it was like the entire world had shifted on its axis. Everything was finally right. Everything finally made sense.

Luke leaned forward and kissed Emmie, hard and deep, before shifting to do the same to Dean, and then he rested his forehead against the demigod's while Emmie stroked both of their cheeks lazily. If she minded still being pinned between the two of them, she sure didn't show it. Luke was glad all over again that his mates weren't mortal with mortal bodies, as Dean had poignantly explained their first night together. What they'd just done, this position they found themselves in now...well, it could have gone very, very badly if Emmie were a mortal woman.

It took him several minutes to find his voice, but when he finally did, all Luke could muster was a hoarse, "Holy hell."

Dean chuckled, the sound low and deep and entirely too sexy.

"I second that," Emmie breathed, sounding almost drunk.

With that, they disentangled themselves and collapsed, all

sprawled across the bed at different angles, but still all touching in one way or another, as if none of them were too keen to be apart, even for a few moments, after waiting so, so long to find each other.

After a few moments of pure, contented silence, Emmie eased up, propping her head on an upturned hand.

"So," she said, voice a little gruff from all of her screams, "do you want the good news, or the bad news first?"

Dean and Luke exchanged a look and with a nod, Luke said, "Bad news first."

"Well, the bad news is that we've got a big meeting with...well, pretty much everyone to discuss Balthazar and Beck and the coming war."

Luke tensed at the reminder of the real world, but told himself that there was nothing they could do to stop it. They could only prepare and face it together.

"What's the good news, then?" Luke asked, reaching out to brush a tendril of silvery hair from Emmie's forehead unable to stop himself.

"The good news," she said with a wicked gleam in her eye, easing forward and pressing her lips softly against his. His cock jumped, already rearing to go again, "is that we don't have to be there for another twenty-nine hours."

CHAPTER
TWENTY-ONE

War was coming. Darkness and blood and death was hurtling for them so fast that it would be upon them before they knew it.

Emmie had been there for the last war with the Dark Ones, but this one was so, so different. She had far more people that she loved involved this time around. People that she couldn't stand to even think about losing.

She shuddered and pushed the thoughts away as she strolled through Empyrean. She'd popped in to check in on Z and Zeus—another item on the to-do list to get everything in place, and this one may just be the biggest challenge of them all. Since Luke and Dean were in the Mortal Plane helping Dalton somehow break the news to all of the supernatural beings that the gods were real and needed their help in an epic war coming down on everyone's heads soon—oh and also that he was, in fact, alive—she'd decided to stick around for a bit and kill some time.

She stopped near a glittering pond not far from Zeus' temple high up on Mount Olympus and lifted her face to the sky, letting the cool breeze ruffle her hair. The air here was so crisp and clean, the perfect temperature, and always smelled like whatever each individual person wanted it to. Right now it smelled like honeysuckle, bringing her mind back to the bath she'd shared with Dean and Luke last night. The honeysuckle-scented bath oils had swirled around them as she'd ridden Luke on one of the submerged benches and Dean had stood beside them, Luke's lips closed around the demigod's cock. Her lips curled and she shuddered at the memory, a wave of desire crashing into her so forcefully her knees almost buckled. Would she ever get used to it? Would she ever not want them both more than she wanted her next breath? She didn't think it was possible.

She glanced towards the island she'd called home for so long, where she'd lived but never *lived*.

"Do you miss it?"

Emmie whirled towards the voice and eyes flying wide. This was one of those whoppers that she hadn't seen coming.

"Zerafina?" Emmie asked, truly shocked. "What are you doing here?" She never left the island. *Never.*

Zerafina looked as she always had, ageless and beautiful, eons of knowledge in her depthless black eyes. She was still sharp and cold, but she looked...wary. Aamon and Magera stepped from behind Zerafina, and Emmie took a step back, her runes flaring and power coiling in her palms, but Aamon raised his hands in a placating gesture.

"We aren't here to harm you Emmeralda—I'm sorry, Emmie," he corrected with a smile. His silver eyes had always been kind and that hadn't changed, even in all these years. "We're here..." He trailed off, glancing to Zerafina for help.

"We're here to help," Zerafina said, shoulders stiff.

"But you can't," Emmie protested, brow furrowed. "The Fates... you don't interfere."

Zerafina raised a red brow, clearly saying *you're one to talk.*

"What is coming is..." Zerafina swallowed hard. "You will need all of the power you can get. *We* will need it," she amended. She exhaled roughly. "We have been removed for too long, have been apart from the world for too long. We have sat back and watched as people suffered and died. Some is necessary, but..." She shook her head, face pinched, and if Emmie didn't know any better, she would say Zarafina looked upset. Upset about the fate of other people, people she didn't even know. *The hell realms must really be freezing over right about now.*

"It is too much," Zerafina finished.

"None of us could take it any longer," Magera said, softly, her green eyes so vivid in the glinting sunlight that they seemed to be glowing. "We want to help. We want to fight."

"And after we win," Allister said, stepping out from behind a sculpture of Taylor Swift. Zeus had always thought it was amusing that mortals decorated their homes and palaces and gardens with statutes of the gods, so he decided long ago—after many, many ales —that he would adorn his own realm with statues of mortals he found particularly noteworthy. They ran the gambit from Mother Theresa to Henry Cavill, and everything in between.

Emmie's eyes went wide at the sight of her brother, tears immediately springing and making her vision blur. She hadn't seen him in months and never, ever expected to see him back on any of the godly planes, but especially not here. There was too much bad blood and the remnants of shattered hearts in Empyrean.

"After we win, they want to live," he finished. "*Really* live." He smiled at his sister, warm and gentle as always, but she could see the strain in it. Being back here was hard for him. She'd hoped to spare him from this fight, to beg him to help on the Mortal Plane with all of their supernatural contacts, but not to join it.

Aamon nodded enthusiastically, golden hair sliding over his forehead. "Yes, we've seen what you and Allister have experienced since you left and...Well, we want it too." He sounded a little embarrassed or ashamed to admit it, but after a moment, pushed his shoulders back and held his head high. *Good for him*, Emmie thought.

"And you're here because?..." Emmie asked, giving her twin a hard look.

"They asked me to help, and I knew that you'd beg me to stay out of it. I don't love being back, but we're all needed, Alda, you know it. And you know how much more powerful we all are when the five of us are together." Emmie's heart clenched at the thought of Allister fighting and possibly falling in this war, but she swallowed down the fear. She turned to Zerafina.

"You too?" she asked skeptically.

Zerafina's lips pressed into a thin line, and Emmie's own curled upward at her clear annoyance.

"Yes," Zerafina said simply. She gave Emmie a challenging look, jutting her chin.

"Oh, I'm so going to need more deets on that becau—" Emmie gasped as a vision hit her. A vision of battle, blood and death, but the Fates were there, all of them drawing power from each other and—

"Holy shit," Emmie finished instead, eyes wide. "We take down one of the Dark Ones. The five of us."

"Yes," Magera nodded. "When we saw the thread, showing that we could help end one of them—at least one, maybe more—we knew we had to act. Almost nothing can kill them. Which is why they were imprisoned the first time around, of course."

"So, hence why they begged me to come," Allister said, a smug look on his face. Emmie's brows quirked up in interest and Zerafina bristled. Emmie's eyes widened.

"You didn't!" She grinned.

"I did," Allister shrugged. He'd made Zerafina literally beg him to assist. Gods, she loved her brother so much.

"And as my last act as an official Fate, I hid that vision from you," Zerafina sniffed in Emmie's direction. Emmie felt a tiny, *tiny* twinge of guilt, but Zerafina had been ready to kill Allister when they'd seen the vision of him in love with Hermes, so really, serves her right.

"What will happen to the tapestry?" Emmie asked.

"New Fates have been called forth from the ether. They man the tapestry now. We...we can never return," she said quietly, a tiny tremble in her voice.

"Zerafina," Emmie started, sympathy rushing through her. "I—"

"I made my choice," she said sharply, raising her chin, all traces of regret or fear gone.

"Well, alright then," Emmie said.

"Allister?" a stunned whisper came from behind them. Allister's body went rigid, as if he'd been electrified, the blood draining from his face as he squeezed his eyes shut. After a second he let out a long exhale and opened them again.

"Knew it would happen at some point," Allister muttered before turning to face the beautiful god behind them.

"Hello, Hermes," Allister said, his voice hard and to anyone else, it would seem as if he didn't care at all, but Emmie knew better. She could feel the strain and hurt beneath the words and she itched to reach out and throw her arms around her twin.

Hermes stood there in silence, staring at Allister, his mouth opening and closing like a fish tossed on land. His blonde curls were damp and plastered to his temples, and Emmie realized he must have just come from working out—or a sparring session with the Elite, more likely, Emmie thought when she noted the dried blood on his chin and collar of his shirt. The Elite were Zeus' personal guards, but they liked to rumble with all of the gods to boost their already giant egos.

"Wha—" Hermes had to clear his throat roughly before he could get a full sentence out. Emmie felt horrible for him. What had happened between him and Allister was a misunderstanding and she knew how horrible Hermes felt, how heartbroken he'd been over it, but she'd promised herself—and Allister—that she wouldn't interfere. She'd kept her word...so far, but she had ideas churning. She'd decided that life is too short to waste time on regret and misplaced anger. The world could very well end soon enough. She didn't want either of them to waste another second of their lives being stupid.

"What are you doing here?" Hermes said, voice coming out a bit stronger this time.

"Didn't you hear?" Allister said dryly, "there's a war brewing."

Hermes just stared and it took him a minute before the words seemed to soak through the shock of seeing Allister again after all these years. Hermes' eyes looked glassy with unshed tears and the sight seemed to weaken Allister's resolve. He exhaled long and slow.

"I'll...find you later," Allister said, voice rough.

Hermes swallowed visibly and nodded, and Emmie could tell the god was trying not to let his hopes get too high. Allister turned his back on Hermes and the god went on his way, waving a little awkwardly to the rest of the group.

"Dear gods," Magera whispered. "He's...oh my goodness..."

Allister met Emmie's eyes and she quirked a brow. Allister rolled his eyes.

"If we're going to fight together, I'm not going to be able to avoid a talk. Might as well get it over with now. It doesn't mean anything." She didn't need to tell him that he couldn't lie to her, but she decided to let it go for now because the stone at her throat pulsed gently just before a soft voice caressed her mind.

-Where are you, love?-

As a marriage gift, Hades had imbued three gemstones with power that would allow Emmie, Dean, and Luke to communicate telepathically across any distance, the same way the brothers and their wives could. No one had batted an eye when the three of them had announced that they were getting married and that they were doing it that night. Everyone understood the urgency, the need to declare feelings and cement bonds with a possibly unwinnable war on the horizon.

-Back already?- she responded.

-They needed...time to process everything. I think they'll come around though. We're in Aqueous. Si needed me.-

-No, he didn't- Luke said, and Emmie could practically hear him rolling his eyes. *-Skylar told us to bring Beck take-out from Golden Palace.-*

Emmie laughed, probably looking insane to the former Fates standing around her. They all stared at her like she'd lost her mind, which wasn't completely untrue some days.

-I'll be back soon...feel free to start without me- she said, another wave of lust making her stomach clench.

-Oh, already on that, love- Dean practically purred, sending a flash of an image into her mind: the two of them in the white tiled shower in their suite in Poseidon's palace, Dean behind Luke, Luke's hands braced on the tile, his claws digging in and leaving deep grooves, water raining down on them, pelting them both as Dean leaned forward and planted a kiss on the back of Luke's neck, telling him to get ready...

-You will pay for that one- Emmie threatened, her blood turning to fire. She loved watching the two of them together, loved when one of them watched her with the other, loved when all three of them wound up tangled together in a mess of sweat and blissed-out pleasure. She loved every second with them, no matter what form it took.

-He's such a fucking tease, isn't he?"- Luke added, but his mental voice was hoarse with desire

-Fuccckkk- he added in a low moan, just before the image of Dean arching his hips forward behind Luke slammed into her mind. She bit her lip and clenched her fists at the swift heat that pooled in her belly at the sight.

-Not fair!- she whined. She felt Dean wink down the connection, and it shimmered closed.

Emmie closed her eyes and took a deep breath, forcing herself to remain here and not phase immediately to join them in the shower. After a few deep breaths, she opened them again and faced the group.

"Husbands," she said with a shrug, as if that explained everything.

As Emmie looked at the group, she felt hope surge up in her chest

202 • K. D. MILLER

like a flame. With them here, they stood an even better chance of winning this war. Already mates and matches were being found, marriages and bindings making everyone stronger—Hades and Skylar, Poseidon and Beck, Dalton and Aphrodite, herself and Lucas and Dean...maybe even Allister and Hermes again? Zeus and Zahara, Ares and a mystery woman Emmie could only catch hazy glances of, Hera and a saucy red-head shifter that Luke would soon introduce her to, Medusa and Hercules, Lilly and another mystery man that Emmie couldn't quite see clearly...So many possibilities, so many stories of love coming together.

It was one thing that the Dark Ones never understood, could never understand: love has power, *true* power, unlike anything else in all the worlds. It was an old, interminable magic that had been woven into the threads of the world before the world even truly existed. Maybe, just maybe, it would be enough to win this war.

Things were still shifting, a million different decisions influencing a million different threads of the tapestry, but Emmie clung to hope with both hands, letting the fire burn through her veins. They had a real chance. They could do this. Together, they could save everything.

A slow smile lifted her lips.

Bring it on, bitches.

Acknowledgments

As usual, this book wouldn't have been possible without a whole host of people, so I need to thank:

- My husband, for always supporting me in this crazy hobby no matter how many times I say "oh, I need to more <insert book-writing/publishing related thing here>!" You are the best. I like you and I love you.
- Lexie, Kayleigh and Kala, for being my nonstop cheerleaders (and sometimes bullies...)
- My amazing PA, Nancy, who I couldn't survive without!
- All of my readers who keep coming back for more. I think maybe there is something wrong with you...but I'm very glad for it! 😄

ALSO BY K. D. MILLER

Adult Contemporary Romance

- Carpe F*cking Diem
- Wrong Place. Wrong Time. Right Viscount.
- Puck the Holidays (Vipers Sin Bin - Book 1)
- Puck of the Irish (Vipers Sin Bin - Book 2)
- The Pieces You Kept

Adult Paranormal Romance

- Red
- Dark Burning (Veracity of the Gods - Book 1)
- Sweet Tempest (Veracity of the Gods - Book 2)
- Vows Forged in Blood

Young Adult Sci-Fi/Fantasy

- Titan Rising (Outliers Series - Book 1)
- Titan Unleashed (Outliers Series - Book 2)
- Titan Reckoning (Outliers Series - Book 3)
- Evansfire